Dead Jokes

Mark Brennan

For all my fellow jokers

Chapter 1

Anna watched a viral video of her husband dancing himself to death while an elderly woman reminisced about her late husband. It was easy to hide the phone in her notebook. Nearly everyone in the widow's support group brought some kind of journal to the meetings. These ladies recounted the long lives of partners lost to old age, while Anna grappled with sudden loss.

Part of her wondered if a group geared toward younger widows might've been a better fit, but it'd been hard enough to open up to this group—most of whom couldn't remember her name. Plus, there was something about the group's facilitator she liked.

The composition book was more than a cover for her phone, however. It was a journal she'd kept since Graham had died. Every session, Anna ignored the other mourners as she jotted down things she missed about him, as well as those she resented—oftentimes, one and the same.

Sensing another long story wrapping up, she locked her phone and pretended to pay attention. Disengaging entirely would have been rude, but the old bats were pretty much oblivious, so Anna multitasked. Sometimes this multitasking entailed staring blankly at the tasteless beige walls of the rec center conference room or nodding absentmindedly.

Before closing the journal, Anna glanced at the clipping of his obituary. As she often would, she ruminated on the phrase describing her—Graham was *survived by* his wife and their two sons. The use of that word was so glib. Because she and her children didn't die, he'd somehow survived?

No. Graham was not *survived* by anyone. He was dead. Gone. Forever.

After he died, there'd been an outpouring of sympathy from the farthest reaches of their combined families' social footprint. Close relatives, second cousins, cousins once removed (whatever that meant), old coworkers, current coworkers, Graham's coworkers, college friends, the boys' friends, parents of the boys' friends, long-lost friends—even the mailman and Graham's barber stopped by and sent a sappy card. Anna was flummoxed by the circling of so many wagons.

But after the funeral, the fanfare ended as suddenly as the love of her life had been plucked from existence. The wagons packed up and moved on. Close friends and family had all done their part to help, but it was time to pick up where they'd left off. Even her sons, Alec and Neil, who undoubtedly shared her sadness, let their daily calls and texts taper off. Anna found herself alone in an empty room while the rest of the world put Graham's death behind them. And it pissed her off.

Their sympathy felt fake now. As though they hadn't reached out for her benefit at all—like it'd always been for their own peace of mind. If any of them truly cared, they'd be struggling through every single day—every hour—the way she was. But they all shrugged and went back to business as usual.

Fucking assholes.

Hearing strangers share similar sentiments about husbands they'd lost did little to validate her grief. On the contrary, their stories made hers feel absurd. Still, this was Anna's third week with the widow support group, and she hadn't yet told her story. This time, after another story that sounded just like the one before it, she raised her hand.

"Anna, thank you—please share with us," Beverly, the facilitator, said. "Today's theme is the *worst*. So, what has been the hardest for you?"

Her face twisted in a stifled cry. "Everything," she whispered, then took a long, hard breath. "Even the bad stuff. He'd leave his towels on the disgusting bathroom floor, and then reuse them the next day. The fridge was always full of rotting leftovers because he hated to *waste food*."

This drew chuckles from the other seven mourners. Most of them were in their sixties or beyond. Anna couldn't equate their pain with hers, having lost her husband and the father of her young adult children long before his time. *Your husband lived a long life*, she'd think. *Suck it up!*

After a few more anecdotes, Anna looked around to see moisture in the eyes of every woman in the circle. A few dabbed their noses with overused tissues.

"Graham is—well, *was*—a compulsive prankster," she said, pausing. "To be honest, he pissed us all off—me and my two sons. He'd hide around any and every corner for minutes on end, just to be able to scare us out of our skin."

The women laughed. Anna blinked back tears. She'd only given them a snapshot of who her husband was, and they were charmed. But she'd shared a life with him for nearly two decades, and her love for him was painful even before he died.

"He just couldn't help himself. I always said it was his love language," Anna said, fiddling with the ball of overused tissue in her hands. "I know he did these things to his friends and coworkers all the time, too—but only the ones he really liked. And if anyone ever got him back, he would never get mad. It's like he was flattered by it."

Beverly acknowledged Anna's struggle to keep her composure. "One of the hardest things about grief is appreciating the things we took for granted when our loved ones were alive. I've had trouble sleeping without my Howard's snoring ever since he passed. And it's been over a year."

Anna laughed and cried in a single gesture. "Is that supposed to make me feel better?"

"No," Beverly said with a kind smile. "It's only meant to make you feel heard."

"Thank you," Anna whispered as she nodded. "Sleeping is hard for me, too. The bed feels so big and empty without him. I think too much and fall asleep too late. And when I do, I have nightmares. I even sleepwalk. I thought that was a myth, but now I wake up somewhere in the house, holding a random object. It's a different world for me now."

Other ladies nodded, and Beverly thanked her for sharing. "It's a different world for us all. One we never could've imagined, even if we saw it coming."

The session resumed with the next grieving wife's account of her dead husband's isms, but Anna blankly stared at her own fidgeting knees. She needed to get out of here and cry, but leaving abruptly would be a faux pas. Instead, she nodded or shook her head when the others did until time was up.

The drive home after these group meetings was always agonizing. Anna had told herself more than once that this support group wasn't right for her, but one of the redeeming qualities was the cathartic meltdown she'd have in the car afterward. It sucked—Anna saw it as little more than emotional vomiting. And just like puking, no matter how miserable it was, refraining from it was worse.

Today would be a monumental purge.

She'd shared a scant sample of what made Graham the man she loved. There was so much more. But even her sparse account of him had opened the floodgates, and she wondered if the deluge would ever end.

Chapter 2

At home, Anna collapsed on the carpet with her hands over her face, sobbing though the tears had run dry.

She struggled with the romanticism associated with her husband's death. Up until the last day of his life, they'd had conversations that took a toll on their marriage. Bills, chores, social obligations, parenting styles—her mature attention to these things contrasted with Graham's laissez-faire approach. They talked about marriage counseling for years, after the most bruising arguments.

Their grown sons had also clashed with Graham on touchy topics. In the end, none of them had chosen the right last words to say to him. Quite literally, he'd gotten the last word. With the simple act of dying, he'd made each of them the real asshole in their respective stories.

And he would've found that hilarious.

Graham was far from perfect—as a husband, as a father, and in many other respects. In fact, his fallibility as a construction worker was what ensured his demise. Still, his flaws—fatal and all—were absolved over the course of his absence. It no longer mattered he'd had an addiction to sports betting, or that he'd once raised his hand at

Anna in anger. The boys would inevitably forgive him for never saying the words "I love you" to them, even though Anna knew it bothered them.

She wondered how much of this Graham thought about on his fall from the twelfth-story roof. Anna had done her research—his journey to the pavement would've been about a second and a half long. What went through his mind?

The man of their house would place a bag of ping-pong balls in the kitchen cabinet, and carefully pull the bag out through the ajar door, keeping the balls stacked inside. Then, in the morning, the unfortunate sap who made the first bowl of cereal would endure a cacophony of plastic orbs bouncing incessantly across the kitchen floor. Graham wouldn't even be there to witness it, yet it somehow gave him satisfaction.

Once, he created a devious contraption to torment Anna and the kids, and used it for years. He took a long, narrow, plastic stick—designed to feed electrical wires behind sheets of drywall—and affixed a hawk feather to the end. With the device's ten-foot reach, he could tickle the ears of anyone in the house from across the room, or even from around corners. No one in the household was safe from an ear tickle at any point in their existence.

But these sins would never be lambasted. Instead, they'd be celebrated. Enduring such relentless tomfoolery required a level of desensitization over many years. Letting that go was no easy task.

At the next support group meeting, Anna needed to show the other ladies why her grief was so different from theirs. She volunteered to share her thoughts.

"My Graham was a joy in my life—our lives—and nothing I say makes that untrue. *But . . .* he sort of gave us all PTSD." A few snickers arose from the others at her reference to the post-traumatic stress his pranks caused them. "He always joked that no one would ever sneak up on his family, because we were so conditioned to peek around corners and look over our shoulders every few seconds. Even when he was nowhere near home, I'd nudge the door open with my foot before peeking into a room."

When the group's laughs faded, Beverly spoke. "And you miss this now, is that right?"

Anna looked upward pensively. "No . . . not yet, anyway, because I still do those things. Graham's been gone for almost a month now, and I've sat in my desk chair numerous times since. But every time, I still check underneath first, to make sure it isn't rigged with an air horn."

More laughter, while Anna forced a smile. They didn't understand. Just because it was humorous didn't mean it wasn't serious.

This reminded her too much of the eulogy she gave at Graham's funeral. It was impossible to celebrate who her husband was without reflecting on his penchant for shenanigans. She'd tried to convey this to a crowd of mourners who couldn't truly grasp what she and her sons had lost. Perhaps they took her anecdotes as attempts at levity, but knowing that she'd never again be jarred out of her skin by a lurking Graham epitomized her sorrow. She hoped those attending out of obligation had understood better when she broke down in uncontrollable sobs while everyone else was laughing.

"I have PTSD because every time I check around a corner or look for him creeping up behind me, he isn't there," Anna said, her voice quivering. "I'd give anything to live with that fear again."

Anything.

Chapter 3

Anna's cry in the car after the support group session was too intense to attempt driving. Her tears flowed steadily enough that it'd be like navigating a monsoon without windshield wipers. After fifteen minutes of sustained weeping, she decided it was safe to try making her way home. But before she could back out of the parking space, someone tapped on her driver's side window.

Anna dabbed her eyes and nose and rolled the window down. "Hi, Beverly."

"Sorry if I startled you," she said.

Anna chuckled. "Please. It takes a lot more than that."

Beverly smiled, then held up Anna's composition book. "You left this next to your seat. I only looked through it enough to be sure it was yours. Figured you'd want it back."

Anna snatched the journal. Her aggression felt rude. "Sorry, I—it's just that it's kinda personal. Private ramblings and stuff."

"Of course. My apologies."

"No worries," Anna said, wishing the statement was true. "I

wrote down a lot of Graham's stupid pranks and stuff. As much as he pissed me off with that shit, I don't want to forget it. If that makes any sense."

Beverly smiled. "Makes perfect sense."

"Not much else does these days," Anna said.

"I know this is a bit forward," Beverly said, "but would you mind joining me for a cup of coffee? Or maybe lunch? A midday cocktail? Whatever you're up for."

This was unexpected, and Anna didn't have an excuse. She tried to conjure one up, but drew a blank. Then, her shoulder twitched. It wasn't like a convulsion or tremor as much as a sensation of being nudged. And she hadn't had a drink in forever. She followed the whim.

"You know, a glass of wine sounds amazing right now, Beverly. Where do you suggest?"

"Call me Bev. Beverly is my government name," she said with a broad smile. "That's what my Howard always told people. His friends called him Cowboy. If anyone called him Howard besides me, he assumed he was in trouble. Anyway, I have a friend who runs one of those wine and paint joints right down the road. We don't have to do any painting, and the wine might even be on the house. How's that sound?"

Anna stared straight ahead, waiting for an excuse to pop into her head. *But why?* Lately, she didn't leave the house because the idea of being around undevastated people repulsed her. Beverly served as a reprieve from such normalcy.

She nodded. "Yeah, I think I am. But can I ask why you're inviting me, out of everyone?"

With a coy smirk, Bev said, "Let's discuss that when we get there."

"If you insist," Anna said, offering a cautious smile. "I'll follow you."

Beverly got into her big Buick, and Anna tailed her to a strip mall occupied by small businesses. She spotted the segment with a sign reading *Vineyard van Gogh,* correctly assuming it was their destination. The pair emerged from their cars to go inside. Beverly held the door with a genteel nod at Anna. "Ladies first."

Inside, a trio of early-thirties, well-to-do women giggled, glasses of white wine in one hand and paintbrushes in the other. Whatever they were laughing at, Anna was certain it wouldn't be funny to anyone but them.

Bev shot a look over her shoulder and mimed gagging herself. "There's a *type* that comes here. But don't worry—we can sit far away."

The three basic bitches sat side-by-side, painting their novice creations. One was a puppy, the other a teddy bear holding a Starbucks cup, and the third was indiscernible. They leaned on each other with hysterical laughter, as if this was the most entertaining experience they'd ever had.

Another woman emerged from a back room—where she presumably hid from the obnoxious display on the main floor. Normally, the painting process would be guided, but with women this drunk, the proprietor most likely threw in the towel on any semblance of order.

"Bevvy!" The black-haired, rosy-cheeked woman trotted around the short bar to give Beverly a warm hug. "Thank you so much for coming," she said, flashing wide eyes at her friend. Anna inferred the women at the other end of the establishment were just as unbearable to her.

"Well, where else could I find a decent bottle of wine this time of day?" Bev said. She gestured her open hand at Anna. "I'd like you to meet my friend here, Anna. She recently lost her husband as well."

The pretty woman offered a wave, rather than stretching awkwardly across a wide table for a handshake. "Good to meet you, Anna. I'm Cary. So sorry for your loss."

Before Anna could acknowledge this, Bev groaned. "People need to stop saying that. *Sorry for your loss,*" she said, then stuck her tongue out in disgust. "It's so cliché. Unless you killed my loved one, don't say you're *sorry*. And if you *did* kill my loved one, you can shove your sorries in a dildo and go fuck yourself."

Anna and Cary broke out in laughter. The insufferable three at the other end of the bar stopped their squealy giggling and shot them a harsh look. Anna didn't know what exactly was happening here, but it felt right.

Chapter 4

Two hours and three glasses of buttery chardonnay in, Anna learned a lot more about Bev than she had in the grief support group they attended three times a week.

Bev and her late husband Howard had met in jail in the 1970s, after getting busted at a Black Panther basement gathering. Upon their release, Beverly fled from her racist family to elope with Howard, who'd left Atlanta behind to build a life with her. They were married by an Elvis impersonator in Vegas during the mid-1980s and lived happily in the Smoky Mountains of Tennessee until their retirement.

"The typical American love story," Bev joked.

Howard's pension was meager, so they moved to Wyoming, where their dollars held more value. They raised chickens, goats, and kept two old horses on a small ranch, paying taxes and insurance with the proceeds they made from the local farmer's market, until years later when Howard was diagnosed with Stage IV colon cancer. At that point, they relocated to Minneapolis to be close to the Mayo Clinic, where he'd get the best care available. Bev helped him fight for nearly a decade before he succumbed to the disease.

Cary shared her own experience with loss, whispering to keep the details out of the tipsy bitches' earshot. At thirteen, she'd found her father dead in the bathtub—bloody and nearly headless from a self-inflicted gunshot wound from a .50 caliber Desert Eagle pistol. She recounted trying to scoop his brains away from the drain, in case he could be fixed. The story left a pit in Anna's stomach just as the spotlight shone on her.

"Do you want to tell us what happened to Graham?" Bev said. "It's okay if not. You might not be ready. You haven't had much time."

In the group, Anna would've declined this solicitation. But here, with an audience of two, and three overfilled glasses of smooth wine coursing through her system, she figured *why not*.

"Sure," she said, spinning a coaster. "I'm ready."

But was she? Part of her mind said to clam up, but the semi-drunk section of her brain said to ignore that part. After all, she couldn't avoid talking about what happened forever. Gut-wrenching as it might be, she'd have to come to terms with it at some point. Not to mention, there was video footage out there that held the truth. The internet would never forget it.

And neither would she, watching it as often as she did. At least twice when she woke up, three to five times while she ate meals, and anywhere from once to a dozen times before going to sleep.

It was death footage, and therefore banned from most platforms. Still, in a Valium haze one night, Anna had searched hard enough to find it in the web's dark corners. Seeing it for herself had broken her heart and scarred her forever; but she didn't regret watching it. In a way, it made him stay with her—tattooed a permanent place for him in her mind.

Graham had gained a meager following on his coworker's TikTok account for performing a dance called the *Griddy*. This move called for the person doing it to alternatingly tap their heels, either in place or while walking, while swinging their arms back and forth. Over a dozen videos included Graham doing the Griddy on a steel beam above the Minneapolis skyline, each of which had something in the range of a hundred reactions. The last, which captured the demise of the husband and father of two, flaunted an insulting two million views. It'd been reproduced so many times it had been immortalized.

Graham's death had gone viral.

He was a damn fool, and she knew it when she married him. But when they had kids together, she saw Graham as more than just a man-sized version of a fourth-grade class clown. He knew how to love. He was a leader. He stayed up for days at a time to handle their first son's acid reflux, when Anna was ready to shake the baby to death. He did it again when their second son couldn't tolerate breast milk—he'd even sold his baseball card collection and Barry Sanders rookie card to help fund the premium formula required to satisfy his youngest boy's dietary needs.

That was who Graham was. But he was also the guy to do the Griddy on a steel beam 120 feet above the concrete, solely for the amusement of the guys around him. He'd done it at least thirteen times before. So why not one more time? Or a hundred? Why not make a goddamn tradition of it? It made people laugh, and thus to Graham, it was worth it.

He didn't care about the views, the reactions, the shares, or the viral notoriety. And his coworkers might not laugh every time. The joke was getting old. Yet, no matter how tired they grew of his antics, it made them flash their teeth.

All Graham ever strived for was a laugh. And it killed him.

Drug lords, crooked politicians, and Elon Musk would continue drawing breath in Anna's world, despite all of them deserving a long and painful death. But her modestly imperfect man died on camera— a sick circus spectacle—because he wanted the people around him to chuckle.

The care packages left on her doorstep had urged her to trust in the almighty God. *Here's a clump of flowers. Trust in Him.*

Fuck you, Karen. There is no justice.

Not in this lifetime, anyway.

Chapter 5

Bev and Cary listened to Anna's account of Graham's death, enraptured. All their stories of loss were sad, but Anna's was fresh, and raw. She wiped her lips.

"I watch that damn video, and every time I still hope he'll be okay. Even though I know what's about to happen. I wish I could just reach through the screen and take his hand. And the Griddy—I see that damn dance everywhere lately. It's so carefree for everyone else. But when I see it, I get a knot in my stomach. I probably always will. Wish it'd go away, for fucks sake."

They paused to sip their wine while Anna gathered herself. She'd broken down before describing the video, and never fully regained her composure. Each time she met Beverly's eyes, she noted a sympathetic and satisfied expression on her face. Without it being said, Anna knew Bev had been trying to elicit this emotion from her in the group sessions.

Anna gulped from her glass before continuing. "The hardest part of watching the video was the look on his face before he fell. In all those videos, he's so carefree and playful, you know? And then he clutches this steel beam with a death grip. His eyes were wide, and I really feel like I could hear his thoughts."

"That's terrible. I can't imagine how hard that is."

"Yeah, well . . . it gets worse."

Bev raised her eyebrows. "Worse than *that?*"

Anna answered with a sigh. "It sucks extra bad, because . . ."

"You can say it to us. We get it."

"Right before he lost his balance, he did this one part of the dance."

Bev glanced at Cary, then back to Anna. "Sorry if I'm reading you wrong, but I can't tell if you're trying not to cry . . . or trying not to laugh."

"Beverly!" Cary shouted, covering her mouth.

Anna burst out in laughter. Her facial expression tiptoed the line between ugly crying and being an AFV audience member cackling at a man hitting his head on a garage door. She wiped the corners of her eyes and took a deep breath. "The last thing he did before he fell was —" She swallowed another laugh. "So, you do this thing where you make your hands look like glasses, and . . ."

All three women choked back laughs. Only when Anna busted out laughing did the others follow. But when Anna uncovered her face, she was clearly crying. Cary and Bev quickly sobered themselves.

"I watch that goddamn video," Anna said with a sniffle. "Again and again, I focus on his face at that last moment, and I can tell what he's thinking right before he drops out of view."

"What do you think his thoughts were?"

"*I've fucked around all my life, and I'm about to find out.*"

Bev shook her head. "I think he probably thought about you. I know you can't imagine that, but it's a documented fact—people who survive moments like that consistently report seeing the face of their loved one when they thought it was a wrap."

Anna snorted as another tear rolled off her cheek and onto the bar. She wiped it with her forearm. "Maybe. I'm just not so sure I'm the one he loved most at that particular time in our lives. The boys, sure. But he and I were fighting a lot. Suddenly, he's quoting the Bible to overrule my input on important decisions. And I lost it on him pretty bad when he woke me up telling me the house was on fire as a sick joke. Plus, money . . . all that shit. We were like any other couple that way."

"But what parts of your life together made you so sure he loved you?" Bev said. "And that you loved him just as much?"

Good question. It'd always been hard for Anna to tell whether Graham loved her more than practical comedy, because he'd go to the farthest reaches of Earth if he knew it'd get a laugh. But for her? She wasn't sure he'd even traverse crosstown traffic to meet up with her. It depended on the circumstances, she supposed.

"I distinctly remember Halloween last year—we went to a party and had a great time together. In some of our arguments, I'd tell him how I missed *that* guy. The man who wanted to make *me* laugh, and no one else mattered."

"What was so special about that party?" Cary asked, slurring.

Anna stared at her glass and snickered. "We didn't really fit in with the crowd, you know? It was some bougie house party my work friend invited us to, and everyone was all stiff and shallow. But Graham didn't hold back—he was dressed in a hotdog costume way too small for him, and he acted a fool. Dancing bad, blurting whatever silly thing came to mind—just being himself. And I loved it. *That* was the man I fell in love with. People were laughing, but we were sure they were laughing *at* him, so we broke off to the front porch and made out like high schoolers. We didn't even have sex that night. But for me, it was almost as intimate." She looked up from her glass. "This is sappy. I'm sorry."

"No, please! This is wonderful," Beverly said. "Is there more?"

"Well, we decided to go home, but Graham wasn't going to leave a bunch of stuck-up assholes like that without disrespecting them in some way—again, the man I always loved. So, there was this really realistic skeleton set up in the front yard, and it had some kind of motion sensor that would make it scream at anyone walking by. On our way to the car, he just grabbed it under his arm like it was his, and threw it in the back of our car. It screamed over and over until he closed the door. I was dying laughing, because he was stone-faced. Just another day in the life of Graham. We still have that thing in the shed out back, and I'll always treasure it."

Bev smiled so wide she squinted. "Graham sounds like a fun guy to be around."

"He is—he *was*."

Anna offered a couple more anecdotes about Graham, thoroughly entertaining her new friends. But after an hour or so, traffic to the wine-and-design studio picked up, and Cary had to tend to her incoming customers.

As they left the establishment, Beverly leaned in a little too close to offer one last parting word of comfort.

"I'm not sure if you're ready for this, but I want to plant the seed in case you're ever interested," she said, deliberate in her diction. "I know someone who might be able to make contact with your Graham."

"Oh, Bev . . . thanks, but—"

"Shh! Let me finish. This doesn't mean bringing him back, or any craziness like that. But you might be able to say one last thing. Or hear one last thing from him."

Anna rubbed her eyebrows and took a big breath. "Yeah, I don't know about all that . . ."

Her disbelief wasn't as simple as she needed it to be. Resisting every explanation of what happened when a person died left a void in Anna's ethos—there had to be *some* explanation. She couldn't just refuse to answer the question.

At least, not anymore.

All her life, this lack of belief had presented no problem. Only now, as she tried to make sense of losing her other half, was she compelled to believe *something*—or else disbelieve. And once she surpassed the point of committing to belief, a plethora of options lurked, vultures eager to tear a piece of spiritual meat off for themselves.

Anna could become Christian, Jewish, or Muslim. She could embark on the journey to be Buddhist or Hindu, or any of the zillion fringe beliefs they all spawned. Or, if she so chose, she could invest her immortal essence in any of a multitude of pagan beliefs.

If she relinquished her doubt, Anna's soul would be up for grabs.

Cary reappeared after getting some customers settled in. She studied Anna and Bev. "Are you talking to her about Theresa? Because Theresa is the bomb-dot-com. Knees of the bees. The cat's lingerie. You name it."

Anna frowned. "Is that right?"

"Most def," Cary said with a hard nod. "I found peace with my dad through her. Closure. Forgiveness. All that. She knows what she's doing."

"Really," Anna said, deadpan. "I don't know if that'll be . . . you know, *helpful* for me."

Bev waved her hand. "Sure. Of course not—not now, anyway. But if you change your mind, and just want to explore your options, all you have to do is text me. Text me and I'll reply, so you have my info."

Anna complied, texting Bev, who then replied with a smiley face, then summoned an Uber. She offered to share it, but Anna declined, saying she didn't want to leave her car in a parking lot. This was the truth. On top of that, she doubted she'd get a DUI in the middle of the day.

As foolish as this choice was—a fact that struck her halfway home —Anna made it without incident. When she walked through the front door, the silence reminded her she had the place to herself. The boys had both moved out and didn't visit as much these days. She could do exactly what she wanted to do, and so she did.

She curled up on the couch and wailed unabashedly into a cushion until her tears ran dry.

Nothing new.

Chapter 6

Dehydration became a real concern as Anna lay on the couch, staring up at the ceiling for the tail end of two hours. She'd cried enough that sobbing produced only sound. Her abdominal muscles hurt as though she'd been laughing for hours. With some vocal self-talk, she found the gumption to sit up.

What now?

She'd gotten drunk, spilled her guts, and cried until she could cry no more. What was the next step in coping with this grief? All that came to mind was whatever her therapist, or Dr. Phil, or Bev might say in response to such a question, and she hated all of it. She took a long, hearty breath, and let it out slowly. The answer fell upon her like a softly settling bed sheet.

Go find that skeleton.

Anna didn't know what good it could do, but maybe coming in contact with an object from her history with Graham might elicit some deeper sentiments—perhaps draw a deeper emotional purge to help her along with her progress in mourning. Sooner or later, she'd have to move on, and she wasn't there yet. But, somehow, she had to get there. The boys still needed her, and all the bills were past due. Her job could only extend so much leniency. She had to get back to functional.

Upon deciding to venture to the backyard shed, Anna realized how intoxicated she was. Putting one foot in front of the other should've been a simple task, but she couldn't do it without great effort.

A summation of life after Graham.

As she stumbled through the backyard, the cool autumn air felt a little colder, like she'd walked into an air-conditioned room. The shed stood stoic, awaiting her. Graham was always the one to go to the shed for things. Anna couldn't deal with the unknown—spiders, millipedes, rats—whatever creepy creatures lurked in that unused building. But now, with a hefty dose of liquid courage in her blood, she marched ahead with authority, undeterred from her objective.

When she reached the shed's door, it was like hitting a force field. She could enter, but only after a moment of reflection and a mustering of inner strength. *The spiders won't bite me*, she recited in her mind. *There's nothing in here that I should be afraid of*. But she didn't believe herself.

With a final heavy sigh, Anna swung the door open. Immediately, a mass of white fell from above, screaming maniacally. It touched her and bounced away.

"Jesus fucking no!" she shrieked, recoiling into a primal defensive stance.

The attacker had flashing red pupils within dark circles for eyes. As the plastic bones swung harmlessly to rest, Anna realized what'd happened. She looked up at the shed's rafters to see the Halloween skeleton's riggings. The whole setup fit a familiar, devious profile.

Graham.

He'd scared her stiff . . . from the dead.

Part of her resented the satisfaction this would give him. But a bigger part appreciated the extension of his existence in her life. He couldn't have known he'd die before the next Halloween. This trap had been set despite the slim odds he'd be there to bask in the hilarity. That was the thing—he never cared if he'd be there to savor the moment. The prank occurring was the sole reward compelling him to do such things.

Sure, he probably smiled as he walked away from the trap he'd rigged, fantasizing about the outcome. But was that enough? Just like the ping-pong balls in the cabinets, this gag came to fruition in his absence, as he knew it would. So why even bother to do it?

Because he was Graham. That's why. Passion propelled him—outcomes were secondary.

Anna dropped to a crouch, breaking into a mournful sob. The skeleton vacillated innocuously overhead while she tried to grasp its meaning in the greater scheme. The scent of sawn pine and damp funk put a pin in this moment—one that would mark her husband's immortality.

Chapter 7

Sunday evening, Anna's youngest son, Alec, texted her to invite himself over for dinner. As usual, he did so under the guise of wanting to check in on his mom, since he lived five minutes away—but Anna knew him well enough to know his primary motive was a home-cooked meal.

Alec had been eager to move out as soon as he graduated from high school, but had no aspirations of attending college. He often joked at his own expense that his big brother Neil was the smart one, and referred to himself as a *Dumb Alec*. He was the only one to weaponize his name in such a way, even though (or perhaps because) there was truth to it. Neil going to college had always been a foregone conclusion, and was now in his second year at Case Western Reserve University, pursuing a medical degree.

While Neil's motivation to leave the nest was academic, Alec's was much more emancipatory. His relationship with Graham hadn't been great, even though (or perhaps because) they were so similar. He butted heads with his father regularly, swearing he'd move out the minute he could—and he'd kept his word. He'd landed a welding apprenticeship and saved his meager income to room with a buddy in a cheap apartment within weeks of high school graduation.

Anna, on the other hand, was always close with Alec. He was the baby, of course; but he was also a big help around the house. By the time he reached his teens, he did chores without being asked, because he was a doer at heart. She appreciated this, since the vast majority of routine household duties fell under her purview. But Anna also bonded with him over simple pleasures—a good meal, a cup of coffee or three, or perhaps a jigsaw puzzle or card game.

Now, with her nest emptier than she could stand, her baby boy would always be welcome. Even if he was using her for a hot meal, she was enamored to oblige. As she prepared her highest-rated dish, chicken cacciatore, she imagined how she'd tell the story of the skeleton prank Graham had left behind. Death hadn't magically repaired the boy's relationship with his father, but his fondness grew with every passing day of Graham's absence.

Alec arrived, and Anna couldn't even wait until he sat down to share the story with him.

"That man was a fool," he said, shaking his head. "Wonder what else he has rigged around here. Maybe we should check the Christmas tree for smoke bombs."

Anna threw her head back and laughed. "Oh, God—I forgot all about that!"

One year, when the boys were young, Graham fitted the family's artificial Christmas tree with smoke bombs that went off after the tree was plugged in. He had a working knowledge of electrical wiring, and had wrapped strands of light filament around the fuses of the smoke bombs. They plugged it in, and soon the house was full of putrid smoke. Anna went into a full panic, which the boys mirrored, and ran around the living room in search of her phone to call 9-1-1. She went into the kitchen to find Graham laughing so hard he was mute—her phone in one hand and a small fire extinguisher in the other.

He'd recognized the possibility of the prank causing a serious fire

—but decided to do it anyway. And he was the only one to find it funny.

Anna plated the meals and set them on the table as the two of them recounted that incident. Alec complimented the aroma of the tasty dish, thanking her before taking a bite and grunting with ecstasy at its flavor. They discussed the latest details of her youngest son's life, and Anna shared her sage adult wisdom as best she could. But as Alec chattered about his job, he frowned.

"You with me?" Alec said, waving his hands. "Earth to Mom!"

Anna snapped to, focusing on her son. "Yes! Of course—sorry, I just had a strange thought. I was listening, I promise."

"Is that the truth?" he said with a coy smile.

"Yes!"

Alec wiped his mouth and folded his hands under his chin. "Then what's my new job title?"

Anna froze. It was a pop quiz, and she hadn't studied. "I'm sorry, hon—I just have a lot on my mind."

"I think you need to get help, Mom. I worry about you."

"Don't worry about me, Alec. I'll be fine. I just need some time is all."

He took a long breath and chewed on his lip. "The thing is, Mom, time hasn't done much for you. Since Dad died, you're a space cadet. Neil don't talk to you because you make him worried. He thinks you're losing your shit. And I understand what you're dealing with, but he's not entirely wrong. You haven't been the same."

Anna reached across the table to grab her son's hand. "Alec, I promise I'm good. It's a difficult time, sure, but I'm a strong person. I raised two hard-headed boys to adulthood, and you're both doing terrific. I'm your father's wife. If I wasn't strong, I'd be buried next to him. Trust me, I can weather the storm."

"Are you still sleepwalking?"

"I'm sorry I even told you about that," Anna said, rolling her eyes. "I was exhausted, and it was right after I found the video."

Alec nodded, then sucked his teeth. "Be honest, Mom. How many times did you watch it today?"

"I didn't invite you over to give me the third degree. You can enjoy my meal and enjoy my company. But if you've come here to accuse me of being insane or whatever, well . . ." she motioned at the front door lazily. "There's the way out."

"C'mon, Mom, don't be dramatic. I just worry about you. That's all." Then, Alec fixed his eyes on something behind her. "Let me ask you this. Have you made a pot of coffee since he died?"

She frowned, trying to recall. Her job had granted her a full month of bereavement time—four times the requirement under company policy—so she hadn't had to work. "You know, I'm not sure. I've gone to Starbucks a bunch, but I can't remember if I've made a pot myself or not. Why do you ask?"

Alec snickered with a closed mouth as he chewed, pointing his fork at the kitchen counter. "How sure are you there ain't salt in that sugar bowl?"

She glanced over her shoulder at it and chuckled. "Not sure at all."

"You should check."

"Oh, I will. I'm not falling for that again!"

One Saturday morning the summer after his graduation, Anna and Alec had sat down for their routine cup of coffee before Graham woke. They'd begun their typical morning chitchat, and simultaneously took a sip from their respective mugs—spitting it out, also in unison.

That time, they'd had no choice but to laugh.

But unlike Graham, they'd only find it funny once. Anna got up from her place and immediately sampled the sugar bowl with her finger. She smacked her lips and looked at Alec.

"Sugar."

Chapter 8

After a few more stories over dinner and some small talk over properly sweetened coffee, Alec prepared to head home. He raised his arms to stretch and announced his intentions with his routine catchphrase.

"Welp, it's about time I hit the ole dusty trail."

Anna smirked. "Let me guess—you gotta wake your ass up at five a.m. for work tomorrow."

He feigned surprise. "How'd you know?"

"Guess I'm psychic."

"Aw, Mom. Don't say that! You ain't crazy!"

She rolled her eyes and stood on her toes to kiss Alec on the cheek. He thanked her for the meal, and she thanked him for the visit. He closed the door behind him, and she followed tradition, peeking through the front window to make sure his car started, and that he made it down the road without incident.

Normally, before Graham died, she'd find him and relate how she missed the small things about the boys living at home. Graham would respond with some witty remark, usually about how he missed having three people to play tricks on instead of just one.

With only a quiet and empty house to tend to now, Anna covered her face with her hands and sobbed. Her shoulders quaked, and a part of her expected to feel Graham's big hands grabbing them in consolation. He'd been a jokester, but he'd known how to comfort her. A simpler man might've tried to cheer her up, but Graham was complex, if nothing else. Whenever she'd cry, he'd do little more than *be there.* He'd just stay quiet and touch her in a way that made sure she didn't feel alone.

Now—and possibly for the rest of her life—she'd have to console herself. The house had felt empty after the boys moved out, but this was harder. Now it was *hollow.* She fell to her knees and buried her face in her arms on the couch, wishing she could feel his touch just one more time.

Then, she froze.

Reflexively, Anna swatted at the air around her, but her conscious mind knew there was nothing there. The hair on her arms rose.

Something had tickled her ear.

Her head whipped around, looking for an explanation—*any* explanation. Because if she couldn't find one, only one would remain. One that made no sense.

She stood and paced around the living room, her face wet with tears and her shoulders raised like a scared animal's hackles. There had to be a bug of some kind—a moth, a fruit fly, *something.* There couldn't be *nothing.*

A few minutes passed with no airborne culprit, so Anna determined the only guilty party was her fatigued mind. She hadn't slept properly in days, and a lack of sleep could easily account for hallucinations like this.

Drinking a cup of coffee after dinner certainly wouldn't remedy this, so she went upstairs to the bathroom to take some sleep medicine. After a shower and her nightly routine, the drug kicked in, and she curled up in bed.

It was a king-size bed, but it felt like a barren empire. Her *king* was gone—there was no regal muscle on the other side upon which to rest her arm. No soothing breaths (or snores) to lull her to sleep. The kingdom she'd once shared with the only man she ever loved—and the only man who'd ever truly loved her—was now a wasteland.

Soon blinded by heavy eyelids, Anna's thoughts quieted. She felt herself drifting into the mysterious universe of slumber when she heard Graham's gravelly voice. Not uncommon at times like this. Things he said, or something she might expect him to say. Now, in that netherworld between sleep and reality, he told her goodbye in his usual way.

See you later, crocodile.

Anna heard her own sleepy voice, "After a while, alligator."

Chapter 9

As they'd often been since Graham's death, Anna's dreams were intense and vivid—but beyond recall. With every waking second, the details would dissipate, leaving behind only remnants of her epic experiences. She'd try to make sense of them, like a paleontologist trying to reconstruct the happenings of the prehistoric world based solely on fossil remains.

But by the time she'd brush her teeth, graphic images of the illusions would wash away like the plaque bacteria being scrubbed from her mouth.

This morning, however, a staunch relic of Anna's sleeping fantasy remained. Her dream—or at least the most memorable part of it—had been about Graham. About his fall. She was with him as he plummeted to the ground, wrapping her arms around his neck. It felt like hours passed. He begged her to let go. It made no sense for them both to die. She could hear and feel the rushing wind. She could smell her husband's dank musk after a long day of manual labor.

Worst of all, she could feel him pushing her away.

Anna did her best not to wake up with a crying spell. To stave it off, she took a long, deep breath and headed downstairs. On the way, she resolved to make a pot of coffee. It might be close to noon, but she could ease into becoming a functional human again by starting her day the way she had before becoming widowed. By establishing a routine.

She rinsed out the stained pot and loaded a fresh supply of grounds, taking a moment to savor their potent aroma. Next, she went to the fridge to supply the filtered water. Anna pressed the button to brew, then took a seat at the table for two.

The coffeemaker let out its last loud gurgles before beeping to signify completion of its job, but Anna stayed seated for several minutes at the dinette table, staring out the window at the sunlit world. Everyone out there went about their business, like nothing horrible had ever happened.

The mailman and the garbageman and the whatever-man would navigate their days right outside her door, oblivious to the pit of despair hiding inside these walls. Undoubtedly, they'd all lost someone important. Old Mrs. Glodowski across the street was aged enough to have experienced loss like this more than once. Why—no, *how*—did they continue with life?

Would she ever be able to do the same?

The smell of the freshly brewed coffee reached her nose, like the flowing, tempting aromas of old cartoons, snapping Anna out of her trance to fix herself a cup. She found herself stirring the sugar in for far too long, spaced out in thought about how much she hated all the fake faces she'd seen at the memorial service. She added a robust dollop of creamer from the carton and stirred it in. Then, she took a sip, and her eyes opened wide.

Salty.

Anna went to the sink to spit it out, but her body refused. As if compelled by a defiant force within, she gulped the mouthful of saline java down, triggering a puckered expression on her face. With a bitter glimpse at the sugar bowl, then the coffeemaker, then her mug, she tried to make sense of what her senses told her.

This couldn't be.

She'd just checked last night, and the bowl was definitely filled with sugar. Alec had left without leaving her sight, so he couldn't have switched the sugar out with salt—but beyond that, Alec wasn't a prankster. His honest nature would never allow it.

On top of all this, Anna was certain the house had been empty when Alec left. She'd felt it as deep as the marrow in her bones. Facts were facts, leaving her little room to speculate as she stared at her mug full of brined coffee.

What the fuck.

Chapter 10

Monday was a long day for Anna, despite her still being off from work on bereavement leave. She spent the day watching the clock, eager to attend the widow's group at seven that evening. Bev had to know about the skeleton and the salty coffee, because Anna needed an explanation. The ear tickle might've been in her head, so she planned to keep that to herself—on top of everything else, it sounded too crazy.

She had Bev's number, but this was a matter to be discussed in person.

Mysticism wasn't something Anna had ever dabbled in. As a child, she'd seen *The Exorcist* long before she was mature enough for such content, which forged a permanent fear of the occult. Death was easier for her to cope with than the idea that her dead parents were watching over her. She grew up to be atheist—not out of passionate doubt of an omnipotent creator, or as retaliation against the religion she was raised to commit her soul to, but out of her fear that supernature was a possibility.

If Anna were to be condemned to a lake of fire forever because she was deeply unsettled by the story that the supreme being of all existence had come down to earth—in human form, only to be tortured and slaughtered—as a means to lift an ancient curse set in motion by a quasi-god-snake and a woman borne of the first man's spare rib, then she was willing to take that chance.

Because that story reeked of bullshit.

All she'd ever wanted was to live a happy life as a decent person and share it with someone who appreciated that. To build a family, and raise it with compassionate ideals. Without believing in anything, she'd gotten exactly what she wanted.

And then it was snatched away.

The downside to her agnosticism was that she had no god to be angry at. If anyone deserved her wrath, it was the man she mourned. Instead, Anna shut down, immersing herself in an indefinite sadness.

After forcing down a Hot Pocket for dinner, she decided to leave early for the group. Bev had always been there whenever Anna arrived, so it was reasonable to presume that Bev *always* arrived ahead of time. Her assumption was correct.

"Early bird!" Bev said as she saw Anna enter the room. "No worms, but I got us some donuts."

Anna didn't even feign a smile. "What did you do? Did you go to your psychic or whatever?"

Beverly recoiled. "I'm sorry? What'd I miss?"

"A lot, I'd say. My husband played a prank on me from the dead! Did you go see your medium person, or whatever? Did you use a Ouija board? What kind of voodoo shit did you pull?"

"Slow down, Anna," Bev said, holding her hands up. "Try to understand where I'm coming from, alright? I have not a damn clue what's got you all upset. I just got here a few minutes ago. All I've been doing is setting up the donuts and the coffee urn. So why don't you take a deep breath, sit down, and tell me what's up?"

Anna did exactly that, still quivering from the adrenaline coursing through her. She met Bev's perplexed gaze. "So . . . you swear you have no idea?"

"Honey, I couldn't be more clueless if I was a Crimson Tide fan."

At this, Anna slouched and rubbed her forehead. "I'm sorry, I—you were talking about ways I could talk to Graham, and then . . . well, this morning was the weirdest thing I've ever felt."

"Okay, go on . . ."

"First, I'm not crazy. So don't give me any of that *you need help* talk, okay? I'm asking for help, and I'm asking you. I already have a therapist. Promise?"

Bev held up three adjoined fingers. "Scout's honor."

Anna closed her eyes and sighed. "Alright. Here goes. One of the pranks Graham played on me—on *us*—was replacing the sugar in the sugar bowl with salt. My son came by last night and we were reminiscing about it, right? And he pointed out that I should check the sugar bowl, just to be sure Graham wasn't pulling a gag from the dead. So—"

"Excuse me," Bev said, holding up a hand. "To be sure I understand—you suspect your deceased husband of pulling a prank on you. Is that right?"

"No—well, I mean . . . yeah."

"Go on."

"So I check the sugar bowl. I lick my finger, get a dab on it, and taste it, and it's definitely sugar. Right? Alec—my son—witnessed it. Then he left, and was never in the kitchen without me, which I'm a thousand percent sure of."

"Sugar in the bowl for sure. Got it," Bev said with a hard nod.

"This morning—okay, *noonish*—I make a pot of coffee, and fix myself a cup."

Two other grieving widows walked into the room, drawing Bev's attention. She pointed to the table. "Help yourselves. It's Krispy Kreme donuts and Snow Day coffee."

Anna scrambled to wrap the story up before further interruption, lowering her voice to a near whisper. "So, when I sip the coffee, it's super salty." She shook her head and widened her eyes. "Just like when Graham pulled that stunt on me. And I *know* I was alone in the house. Can you explain that?"

Bev's eyes danced around in thought, then she squinted. "Are you *sure* you were alone?"

"Absolutely! I locked both doors, and all the windows stay locked. Besides, who would sneak into my house and switch out the sugar for salt?"

Beverly raised her eyebrows and cocked her head. "I'll ask again —are you sure you were *alone?*"

Anna stared in a daze at Bev until she had to stand up to greet the rest of the group. But Anna held her hollow gaze on the chair where Bev had been sitting. Her mouth stayed slightly open, her jaw slack.

At this point, she wasn't sure of anything.

Chapter 11

Two new widows joined the circle for Monday night's meeting, which meant the focus was on them and their fresh losses. Before they introduced themselves, they fit a common profile: elderly ladies who knew nothing beyond the unhappy marriages they'd resigned themselves to in their twenties. Now they found themselves alone. In their day, jobs were a status symbol, the commies were coming for them, and faith in Jesus Christ alone held the family together—all that boomer bullshit. The feeble shell of beings who survived this clever branding now took a metal chair and mourned like the rest of them. Anna tried to care, but her mind was too busy trying to fill in so many blanks.

Who'd switched out the sugar for salt? How had they done it? Why wasn't Bev more stymied by the details of that story? Did it even happen the way Anna now remembered it?

Was she losing her mind?

The rest of the meeting was useless. Two old ladies who were knocking on death's door themselves recounted a half-century of memories with the husbands who'd left them by the natural order of life. Bev hung behind after the session to welcome them and ensure they came back. Anna sat in her chair alone, wondering what her next move was.

She went home, with no other logical option, and sat on the couch. However many times she replayed the sequence of events, no viable explanation solved the puzzle. All that kept coming back to her was the way Bev had asked her if she'd been alone in the house.

It wasn't so much a question about the setting or the security of her home as much as a question of her belief. Anna knew this, because it'd made her uncomfortable.

The internet was a dangerous chasm of information, misinformation, and disinformation. But in times of uncertainty, no resource had ever come through as consistently as the great matrix of all human knowledge. There was no doubt that the modern-day Great Library held the answers Anna needed. What mattered most was the question she asked.

An answer of forty-two, without the right question, would not suffice.

After downing a few glasses of wine, Anna got bold with her Google queries. She asked what she needed to know.

CAN SUGAR TASTE SALTY?
DEHYDRATION SYMPTOMS
B12 DEFICIENCY SYMPTOMS
GASTROESOPHAGEAL REFLUX DISORDER
SENSORY DIFFERENCES
PSYCHOSOMATIC PERCEPTION
SIGNS OF PSYCHOSIS
IS MY DECEASED HUSBAND HAUNTING ME?

None of the hits provided valuable information, let alone consolation. Anna's search for logic was a rabbit hole to Crazy Town. She fell asleep with her head on her desktop's keyboard, drooling into its many gaps.

She awoke shivering in the middle of the night, a waffle pattern creased deeply into her forearm and cheek. It'd gotten warm in the house earlier, so she'd turned the heat off, intending to turn it back on before bed. Now, at whatever wee hour of the morning it was, Anna was surprised she couldn't see her breath.

After a stop at the thermostat to turn the heat on, she made her way upstairs. Instinctively, she paused at the top, peeking around the corner. Graham would often lurk behind corners, and only when his mark was oblivious. It was like he had a sixth sense for any unsuspecting souls in his vicinity.

How long would it be before she stopped being so vigilant?

Even in her tipsy haze, she shook her head and snorted a laugh at herself. If Graham could see her now, he might die again from laughter.

As she approached the toilet to pee out the last few glasses of wine she'd drunk, this occupied her conscious thoughts long enough that she involuntarily lifted the toilet seat to check underneath it before sitting.

He got her again.

Graham once bought a ridiculous amount of snap bangs—Pop-Its, they were called—pea-sized, tailed balls of paper with a small amount of explosive inside that popped upon impact or when crushed. They were a legal novelty fireworks product, and extremely inexpensive. So, when her husband bought over fifty boxes from Target—clearing the shelves—Anna had little reason to object. The boys protested, but to no avail. Graham would not be denied.

They knew not to stand in his way when he set his mind on something like this. What they *didn't* know was how he intended to use the snap bangs to torment them. It would lead to years of being startled by them popping at their feet, against the walls, or rigged in various places.

His favorite spot to booby trap was the toilet seat. He'd tape several to the contact points between the toilet seat and bowl, so when his mark sat down, they'd all pop in unison, startling the sitter of the porcelain throne. Once again, he would rarely be present to revel in the fruits of his efforts, yet it brought him such joy that he gave the whole family somewhat of a complex.

Anna was already sitting when she realized she'd checked. As she urinated, she broke out in laughter that escalated until she found herself weeping again, her face in her hands. Never again would she be jolted stiff while peeing.

God, she missed him.

Chapter 12

Anna needed someone on Tuesday morning. As she'd often told Graham, she was feeling *tender*. Many men—husbands especially—might roll their eyes at such a declaration. But Anna had once had it better than that. When she had announced she was feeling emotionally fragile, Graham responded as though she were stricken with a virus.

Are you okay? Is it my fault? What can I do to help? I'm not the bad guy, am I? Did I do something wrong?

For all his faults, Graham had an urgency about him when he knew Anna was in any form of despair. Most importantly, he had sought to ensure he was not the cause of the ill. And that endeared Anna over the years. But at times, once he was exonerated as the cause of her distress, he'd disengage. Back to silly Graham.

He had to be the clown, but could never be the villain.

Anna lived a life in which he was both. He *was* a fucking clown, falling off a skyscraper and splatting onto the fresh concrete because he did a silly dance on a sixteen-inch-wide steel beam. But this also made him the bad guy, thrusting this sorrow upon her and their sons.

Was a laugh more important than them? Apparently so—which made him the true villain in their stories.

She pulled up the familiar web page and refreshed it. Video of her life partner dancing for the camera and putting those finger glasses over his eyes played yet again. If she watched it enough times, it might stop hurting. So she watched it eight times.

No one could understand this conflict. Even Anna's therapist would go on too long about the underlying tensions and resentments in her marriage to Graham, but offer very little in actionable steps to help her cope. Only one person had proven qualified for what Anna needed now.

Undoubtedly, Bev had a day job. Maybe she'd shared it in the group before, but Anna spent enough of the sessions drifting off in thought about Graham, she might've missed it. It didn't matter. Upon waking the next day, she texted Bev.

> Hey Bev, it's Anna. I want to talk to Graham.

As soon as she hit send, Anna regretted it. First of all, who introduces themselves in a text? They'd exchanged numbers, so why wouldn't Bev have her contact info saved? But second—and most importantly—what Anna was asking to do was absurd.

It made no sense, on multiple levels. Anna wasn't a believer in the supernatural. What good would it do to contact her dead husband? If it worked, she'd have to become a believer. If it didn't, she'd be a fool for trying.

And supposing it worked, what would she say to him? There was so much to say—the backlog of thoughts stewing in her mind since he passed was enough to fill a book. How could she sum it up in a quick message?

Sure, she could tell him that she loved him and missed him. And so did the boys. But he knew that. Would there be any purpose in reaching across the great divide between life and death to state the obvious?

She could tell him what'd happened since he died, like updating a loved one behind bars. Mundane details to link the captive soul to his former existence, as if it added any value for either of them.

What Anna really wanted to tell him was that he acted a fool one too many times, and caused immeasurable anguish to the ones he loved most. That he put his compulsion for comedy over his family. That she was furious at him.

But . . . *why?* So he'd learn his lesson, and wouldn't do it again?

Her phone chimed.

> Hi Anna. It's not quite that simple but let's meet up and I'll take you to see my friend Theresa. She's amazing. Are you free tonight?

There was still time to back out. But while Anna wrestled with the reasons to make contact with Graham, she now had to come up with excuses not to. That was much harder. She tapped her reply into the phone and hesitated.

> Of course I'm free. My life is empty. Does this cost money?

A bit dramatic. And a little too personal for someone she barely knew—but it felt good to type it out. Anna erased her maudlin response immediately, instead sending a simple *"Yep."*

> Ok we can meet at that wine and paint place tonight at six, and I'll take it from there

Yes. Take it from there, Bev. Anna wanted nothing more than for someone else to take the reins. Just reading the words felt like letting out a breath she'd held for too long.

Navigating a life after Graham had been exhausting. In the thickest thick of her shock and grief, she had to *make the arrangements* and *get his affairs in order*—two idioms she'd grown to detest.

Red tape was painful enough. Sprinkle in the worst emotional experience ever, and it became nothing less than torture.

Cold, relentless torture.

It was all considered expectation. She'd spread the news of Graham's passing—answered the plethora of follow-up questions, replied with thanks for the condolences, and assured each and every well-wisher there was nothing she needed. Contacted the mortuary to update public records and helped plan the memorial, funeral, and cremation in accordance with Graham's living wishes—which were vague, at best. Had the house, car, and retirement funds signed over to her. Arranged the catering. Bought the flowers. Created a sentimental slideshow. Delivered the eulogy. Filed the life insurance claim. Consulted with attorneys for the wrongful death suit. Applied for bereavement leave from work.

Anna lost the love of her life and inherited a shitty, endless, unpaid job.

Beverly, by contrast, was the only real support Anna had since Graham's death. Having lived through a similar experience, Bev knew what to say and—perhaps more importantly—what *not* to say. She knew that oftentimes the best way to help was to just listen, nod her head, and pass the tissues.

Now, Anna could entrust her with this latest stage of grief. Whatever it meant to talk to her dead husband again, it could be a means to determine whether he was playing practical jokes from the hereafter, or if these mystics were just hocus-pocus, and she needed to change her meds.

Chapter 13

After meeting Bev at the wine-and-design place, Anna rode with her to a big house out on the outskirts of town. They pulled down a long gravel driveway ending in a dirt parking area Anna presumed had once also been gravel. A handmade sign in front of the main entrance advertised psychic consultations, tarot readings, and medium services.

Anna was certain it resembled a house featured in some movie she'd seen, but it was just as likely it existed only in her head. The window frames were all wooden, with paint chipping off even worse than the old coat of white on the siding. It had three floors, the third being small and topped with a steep, conical roof—akin to a church's steeple. The bottom two floors shared a corner with an octagonal rotunda.

Apparently, the clairvoyant biz was lucrative enough to buy a large house on a nice chunk of land, but not enough to pay for vinyl siding or a fresh coat of paint. Or a professionally made sign.

"Theresa is great," Bev said as she put the car in park. "She really struggled during the pandemic because this kind of stuff doesn't really work over a Zoom call, ya know?"

"Is she here? I don't see any cars in the driveway," Anna said.

Bev razzed. "Aw, yeah—she's always home. She doesn't own a car. Shit, I don't think she can drive, come to think of it. But she has a lot of friends, and we all do things for her here and there. Bring her some groceries, prescriptions, whatever."

"How long have you known her?"

"Almost ten years now. Howard hated her. Said she was taking advantage of my vulnerable state. But, like I always told him, it don't matter to me. Coming here and letting her do her tarot readings made me feel better. I was able to cope as I watched him suffer and spend half his life in hospitals and doctor appointments because of my time coming out here. Hell, sometimes it felt like the drive alone was worth it, because I didn't have to do anything or worry about nothing. Just listen to some tunes and zone out, know what I mean?"

"Yeah, I get that."

Bev turned the car off and started to get out, but stopped, shooting a serious look at Anna. "But that isn't to say Theresa ain't the real deal, because she is. You'll see what I mean."

Anna nodded, and they both got out. The expansive silence struck her. There was no traffic out here, no machinery or technology. Just quiet, broken by the faintest wisp of wind and the thunderous slam of the car doors. It smelled of damp grass and old, waterlogged wood—a mixture that propelled her back to some unidentified time in her youth.

A bell rang as Bev pushed through the front door, reminding Anna that this was a place of business. The inside reeked of bug spray and stale tobacco smoke embedded in the walls and floors.

"Hello?" Bev called out. "You here, Theresa?"

A distant voice responded, "Bev? I'm back here, in the study!"

Bev led Anna down a jagged hallway, past a large room full of bookcases and piles of old newspapers and magazines, a musty bathroom, and a small room packed with plastic tote bins stacked almost to the ceiling. The journey ended at the entryway to a large, carpeted space with a big desk in the center.

The glow of computer monitors shone on the small figure hunched behind the desk. As they got closer, the person took a sharper form—an elderly woman of ambiguous ethnicity, wearing a wave cap with a long tail, reading glasses on the tip of her nose, and loose clothes that appeared to be pajamas. A cigarette burned in an ashtray like incense, the ashes inches long.

"Hey there, Theresa. I brought a friend with me today," Bev said, drawing the woman's attention away from her computer screen.

Theresa looked over her glasses at them and puffed the neglected cigarette. "You must be Anna."

Anna smiled. "Wow. You really *are* psychic!"

The joke didn't land. Theresa held her stare, awaiting elaboration, while Bev shook her head.

"Don't mind her," Bev said. "She's never done any readings before."

Theresa pursed her lips, squinting through the smoke at Anna. "Yeah. I can tell."

Psychic, indeed.

Chapter 14

Theresa and Bev chatted for a minute, leaving Anna feeling invisible. She took the opportunity to look around and take in the ambiance.

Candles burned at random intervals around the spacious room, likely contributing to the pungent amalgamation of fragrances. It was cold despite the fire crackling in the fireplace behind Theresa's desk, which came as no surprise—the ceiling stretched up to the second floor, making a large space to keep heated.

A chessboard sat in front of the window to the right, seemingly in mid-game. By the window on the left was a round table made of thick, grey stone. The four chairs around it were brown metal folding chairs—the kind Anna might expect to see in a bingo hall. A dark brown box sat in the center of the table, adorned with gold or brass flair on its edges and corners. It looked to her like a cigar box that identified as a treasure chest.

"Anna," the old woman said, startling her. "Can I meet you, please?"

"Um—yes, of course." She glanced over at Bev, hoping for a clue as to what this meant. "I'm Anna. What would you like to know about me?"

Theresa shook her head and rubbed her forehead. "No, dear. Come closer," she said, dabbing out a cigarette. She held her hands out, palms up. "Give me your hands. That's how I meet people—see who they are. I never trust who people *say* they are. If they don't lie to me, they're probably lying to themselves. I need the *truth* to provide my services."

Anna bit her tongue to keep from yelling *You can't handle the truth!* But based on how her last joke hit, that could result in expulsion from the premises. Instead, she said, "Okay."

When she placed her fingers into Theresa's cold, bony hands, the old woman grasped them and squeezed her eyes shut. Anna expected a shock of excitement, given all the supernatural energy she should have stored up inside herself. But Theresa stayed still, taking a long, heavy breath in through her nose, then letting it out through a small hole in her lips.

She opened her eyes and shook Anna's hands vigorously. "No! You must relax. Take a deep breath and close your eyes—can you do that?"

Anna nodded, and did as Theresa instructed. With her eyes shut, colorful tracers flew in front of her eyes, pulsating as they drifted in random directions. Nothing unusual. But then, without warning, an image of Theresa's face appeared in negative colors. The sensation that the old woman was in her head struck Anna enough that she gasped, opening her eyes. Theresa was looking up at her, almost smiling.

"I've seen enough," she said. "Let's go to the table."

Anna glanced over at Bev, who offered one soft nod. Theresa shuffled toward the stone table, and Anna followed. She looked back to see Bev standing where she'd been, in front of the desk, with her hands folded.

Why didn't Bev come over with her?

Theresa opened the gold-trimmed mahogany box and pulled out

a deck of cards. She shuffled them in a loose toss while staring into Anna's eyes.

"I know you don't believe in this shit," she said with a wry smile. "But that's fine—I like a challenge. You have a resistant aura. You don't believe in much, do you? Because believing in something makes you weak. Vulnerable. Am I reading you wrong?"

Anna frowned. "I'm not sure about that right now. Guess I'd have to think about it."

"I understand," Theresa said, nodding. "You have doubts about the supernatural, so you don't want to give me any feedback. But what you don't know is that such a response *is* feedback. Yes, I make a living tapping into the astral plane. But I'm not stupid enough to rely on one source of information. I corroborate everything in my readings."

"Makes sense."

Theresa laughed, crow's feet forming at the corners of her eyes. "You don't care how the sausage is made! Fair enough. I'll get right to it, then." She pulled a card from the top of the deck and slapped it in the center of the stone table, face up. The depiction was vague, with a skeleton hiding behind an X made of swords. But the word at the bottom was plain English.

Death.

"Fabulous," Anna said, curling her lips and nodding. "Death. Hopefully it's me, and not one of my boys."

Theresa snickered as she lit another cigarette. "The Death card means nothing of the sort. It's upright as you, the querent, see it; but I'm the reader, and for me it's reversed. That indicates you're fighting against a fear of change. But not a new phase of life. You're facing a decision to either stay as you are, and rot away, or take control and embrace a new direction for yourself."

Despite her best efforts, Anna rolled her eyes. "Oh, okay."

"I don't expect you to *believe* anything," Theresa said, wincing through the smoke. "I don't need to be psychic to know you'll leave here thinking everything I showed you and told you was a bunch of horseshit. It's a guarantee. All I ask is that you let me do what I get paid to do. That's my product. You'll leave here with it, and you can do with it whatever you please. Does that sound fair to you?"

"It does," Anna said with a firm nod.

Theresa flipped the next card, and placed it sideways, its top on the right edge of the *Death* card.

The Lovers.

Chapter 15

The deck had to have been stacked. First *Death*, and then *The Lovers*. Anna began suspecting Bev of tipping her esoteric friend off beforehand. Maybe they were in cahoots for some reason. Despite such logical skepticism, she stayed engaged in the reading.

"This means you are in a state of union," Theresa said. "You are linked to a partner. This is neither good nor bad, but an indicator of the present condition of your spirit."

Anna stared at the card. As much as she wanted to believe in some semblance of reason or purpose behind her anguish, this reeked of a ruse. Yes, she'd watched the old woman shuffling the cards as they talked. But that didn't mean there was any substance to the face of a card. After all, like horoscopes, the meaning of these things was intentionally subjective. Cast a net wide enough, and it becomes easy to hypothesize that up means down. Black actually indicates white, and the sun represents a source of darkness and cold.

"Is that what it means while Mercury is in retrograde, though?"

Theresa took a drag from her cig and glanced over at Beverly. She subtly shook her head. "I understand your cynicism, Anna. What I ask of you is to let me finish my reading. If it helps you in some way, that brings me joy and satisfaction. If it doesn't, I hope you find the help you need wherever you look for it."

Anna nodded hard. "Thank you."

After closing her eyes a moment, Theresa placed another card—this time, sideways on the other side of the *Death* card. It landed facing Theresa, its bottom touching the center card.

Five of Cups. A cloaked figure with a bowed head stands among empty cups at its feet. Anna failed to infer any meaning from the image.

"This card is upright, which indicates loss, emotional detachment from something important," Theresa said before emptying her lungs of smoke. "This is not mystical in nature. Of course you feel this way."

Without another word, she flipped the next card and placed it. *Three of Swords.* It landed inverted as Anna saw it but upright as Theresa read it.

"This is another one I'd expect to see for a mourner. It tells me you're in a consuming pain, and you need healing."

"Makes sense," Anna said with a nod.

"*But*—it's worth mentioning that an underlying message is that you're at a crisis point, or a decision in your path, where you can continue as you've been, or seek a much more challenging spiritual growth. Take from that what you will."

Theresa flipped the next card.

Justice. Upright as Anna saw it, but inverted to Theresa.

"Hmm," the old woman said. She glanced over at Beverly, then peered hard at Anna through the plume of blue smoke. "Is there something you're not sharing with me? Or maybe leaving out when you divulged your feelings to the support group? It seems there's a mistruth within you that's scrambling the frequencies of your life force. I sensed it when you walked in here. It would behoove you to be honest with me during this reading, Anna."

Anna scowled. "Are you accusing me of something?"

"I'm reading the cards."

"How *dare* you!" Anna looked at Bev as she stood up. "I didn't come here to be accused. This is bullshit. Can we go now?"

Bev looked at Theresa, unsure. "It isn't done, though." She looked back at Anna. "Can you just let her finish her reading? I know it isn't easy, but you won't regret it. Anna. Think you could see it through?"

Anna sat and crossed her arms. "Fine. But let's get this over and done with."

Theresa raised an eyebrow as she pulled the next tarot card from the deck. She lost control of it, causing it to fling in Beverly's direction, flipping end-over-end as it floated down. "Ah, shit!" she yelped.

The three of them scrambled to spy how the card landed. Anna spotted it first and shouted what she saw.

"*The World?* The fuck does that mean?"

Theresa, being decrepit, arrived last to see the card as it lay. She frowned. "I'm afraid we'll never know—the meaning is diametrically opposite, depending on the card's orientation to me. I'm so sorry I fumbled the card so carelessly. I won't charge you for this part of the session."

Anna grabbed the old woman by her bony shoulders. "I don't care about the money! *What does it mean?*"

The woman shook her head. "I can't tell you that. How it lands on the table means everything. I could only speculate."

"Then *speculate,* God dammit!" Anna said, shaking her hands in front of the old lady.

She glared back at Anna. "Very well. But please mind your tone with me. This is my home."

Anna lifted her open palms over her head. "I'm sorry. This is a very hard time for me, and I'm a little wound up. Just tell me what the card means, please."

Theresa took a deep breath. "Well, the World card is complicated. Upright, it means you've achieved fulfillment and harmony— or that you soon will. Inverted, however, it indicates that you're suffering from incompletion, and you're struggling to find closure.

Either way, an important part of your journey through life is ending, and a new one must begin."

"So?"

"So, you have to read the card for yourself. I can't tell you which way it was going to land. But you should know. Personally, I have a guess. But it's your card."

Anna frowned at the old woman. Her answer was passive-aggressive, and wholly unhelpful. "I think I'm close to harmony."

Theresa shrugged, then shot a look at Beverly. "Okay, then. I guess that's that. Are we still interested in connecting to the recently crossed-over husband? I'm afraid I'll have to charge for that, though—unless, of course, I screw *that* up!"

She and Bev laughed. Anna sat back, stone-faced.

Very funny.

Chapter 16

While Theresa collected candles and talismans comprising some of the clutter in the big room, Anna stayed seated with Bev.

"I know this place looks like a pigsty," Theresa said with her back turned. "But I know where everything is. Much like the stars, there is order hiding in the chaos."

As the old woman continued mumbling out of earshot, Anna leaned over to Bev. "This is silly, and I think it's triggering me," she whispered.

Bev whispered back, "Trust me—everything triggers you for the first few months. Reserve judgment until you've had a couple days to let it all sink in. When you're not so reactive."

Theresa meandered back, a cache of candles and trinkets cradled in her arms. "I haven't used my channeling devices in quite some time, it seems. I need to find my crystals before we begin, so please bear with me. Would either of you like something to drink?" She let the candles and charms clatter onto the table.

Anna shook her head. "I'm good."

"If you have any more of that Sioux City Sarsaparilla, I'm always ready for a bottle of that," Bev said.

"I'll check the fridge."

As Theresa left, Anna leaned over to Bev again. "I don't know if I'm ready for this—you know, emotionally. How can it help me? What if Graham talks to me through her? What do I even do with that?"

Bev chuckled. "You got the jitters, is all. I get it, believe me. But it's not like the movies. Graham ain't gonna give her a message to deliver to you, like that movie *Ghost*. It's more . . . I can't explain it. But it helps, once you let it sink in. You'll see."

"I'm just—it's already freaking me out that there was salt in that damn sugar bowl. I don't feel like I need to be connected to the astro plane, or whatever. How is this supposed to help me get through this?"

"You have to face it eventually," Bev said. "No one ever thinks they're ready until they make a choice to become that way."

Theresa reentered the room, set her handful of carefully crafted crystals on the table, then slid the bottle of sarsaparilla in front of Bev. She reached into the pocket of her pajamas adorned with cats in spacesuits to produce a bottle opener. "They're not twist-off. Remember what happened last time."

Bev laughed as the two of them recounted a recent incident in which Bev tried to twist the cap off the pop-off bottle and tore the meat of her palm open. Anna forced a smile and chuckled along, but the story was far funnier to the two women who'd experienced it.

"Okay, then," Theresa said, arranging her small army of candles around the table. "This arrangement has to be very specific, and I'm not gonna claim I know why. All I know is that it's worked in the past, and I haven't figured out which little things mattered—because I'm not patient enough to be a scientist—but I know that it works if I do it this certain way."

Anna appreciated this. The signaling that Theresa wasn't omniscient reassured her that there was still some unknown, even among those who claim to have supernatural powers. It was comforting that, at the very least, this woman didn't purport to be a deity, or even a prophet.

Theresa shifted the dozens of candles to various points near the perimeter of the stone table, adjusting them to the half inch or so. After a studious survey of their placement, she arranged crystals of varying colors at intervals closer to the center of the table. Again, she adjusted their places to her precise specifications.

The end result was a smooth, grey table with concentric circles of candles and crystals, the colors forming a spiral pattern. Then, for an anticlimactic pièce de résistance, the old woman turned and lifted a black obsidian pyramid from a hidden spot under the desk. It was about a foot tall, and mirrored the shape of the Great Pyramid of Giza, except it had only three outward sides. She struggled with its heft, setting it on the edge of the table before hoisting it for one thrust over the candles and crystals, onto the table's center.

She straightened her spine, pushing her hands into the small of her back. "Heavier than I remember," she said with a groan. Theresa then turned the pyramid so that each point rested in the direction of each chair at the table. "Shoulda remembered to put this heavy bastard in place first."

Bev popped the top off her soda bottle and took a gulp. "Next time, just let me know if you need some muscle!"

Theresa ignored the comment, focusing on twisting and shifting the pyramid into a precise position. Once it was set, she pulled blinds down over the windows at each end of the room, shrouding them in darkness. Only the dim overhead light and the glow from the computer screen provided ambient illumination. Theresa turned the lights off, as well as the computer monitors.

She began lighting the candles, one at a time, counterclockwise, luring her guests into a meditative trance as they watched. As each tiny flame licked the air, Anna released her doubts. Those loud voices in her mind went silent. The calming scents of fragranced wax and root beer pulled her out of her body. Whatever would happen next, she was ready for it.

Bring it on, she thought. *Make sense of all this.*

Chapter 17

This was a séance, and Anna knew it. Maybe she'd known it all along, but only now did she recognize the scene as the pagan ritual it was.

Theresa lay the back of her hands on the stone table, wiggling her fingers. "Join your hands with mine, please. And your free hands with each other," she said, never opening her eyes. "And you must keep your wrists in contact with the table at all times. The flow of blood through your most vital conduits links the life force of us all to the, uh . . . *afterlife* force—whatever they call it over there."

Anna joined hands as instructed. She felt Theresa's thumb wiggle the wedding band on her left ring finger. Theresa opened her eyes.

"He's touched this. Correct?"

"Who? Graham? Um—I'd say so, yeah. It's my wedding ring."

"Take it off, please."

Anna frowned. "I, ah—I'd rather not, if that's okay."

Theresa raised an eyebrow. "You worry that I'll steal it? That I'll throw it into a cauldron of crow beaks and bat's feet?"

"No—it's just . . . you know, it's hard for me right now. I haven't taken it off since Graham passed. I don't even remember the last time I took it off."

"My dear," Theresa said, smiling through the smoke burning her eyes. "Remember—it's only a piece of jewelry. Looks to be a small amount of gold and a very common crystal. Now, I understand letting go is hard. But it's an essential step toward reaching out. And I assure you, you'll walk out of here with it firmly on your finger."

Anna fought tears for a second, but then pulled her hands together to remove the ring. She handed it to Theresa. "It was his grandmother's. I never met her."

"Well, we may very well meet her in just a moment, if she ever touched it!" Theresa said with a coughing laugh as she looked at Bev, who also laughed. "I'm joking, I'm joking—well, I *think* I am, anyway."

Theresa placed the ring around the apex of the stone pyramid and retook her guests' hands. After a minute or so of meditating—breathing in deeply through her nose, eyes closed, and exhaling slowly through her mouth—she recited an incantation with the same ease as if she were saying grace before dinner.

"*Hear these words, hear my cry, spirit from the other side. Come to me, I summon thee. Cross now the great divide.*"

Anna, whose eyes had stayed closed, now peeked with one eye to see if anything had changed in the room. It hadn't. Theresa and Bev both kept their eyes shut, so Anna reclosed her peeping eye.

After a few more seconds of nothing happening, Anna wondered what she expected to occur. Would Graham appear over the pyramid as a hologram, and profess his enduring love for her? Hold out his finger for her to pull, with that stupid grin on his face? Apologize for leaving her so suddenly, all for the sake of being a workplace clown? Would the table shake, or would a message be spelled out with the many pieces of clutter that filled the room?

She opened her eyes and prepared to announce her intention to leave. This was silly. All that could come of it was more questions. And that's if it was a *success*—whatever success looked like. Imagine failure. Most likely, she'd leave here feeling stupid for coming, because Anna was—or should've been—too rational to dabble in such hooey.

What a moron sorrow had made of her.

As she took a deep breath to make her awkward announcement, the air chilled. Not in the way a fan or vent might blow cold air on her, but a drop in the ambient temperature. No manmade device could produce this. The hair on Anna's arms stood up straight.

"He's here," Theresa said, eyes still closed. "And he knows you feel his presence."

Now, Anna's eyes stretched wide open. Tears clouded her vision until they streamed down each cheek.

This couldn't be.

There had to be some explanation. Maybe Beverly was in on it. Maybe Theresa rigged the climate control in the house to align with the moment she supposedly summoned her lost love. They might've rigged the wiring to produce this jolt of power she felt.

But maybe not.

Anna found herself breathing hard—on the verge of hyperventilation. She glared at Theresa, telepathically demanding her to explain this crippling feeling coursing through her.

"He knows you want to leave," Theresa said, eyes shut. "But he wants you to stay."

Anna blinked another pool of tears from her eyes, struggling to get her next words out. "I don't believe you."

"He wants me to pass a message to you."

Anna's breathing hitched. "I don't believe you."

Theresa called out words as if she were reading from a cue card. *"The skeleton was hilarious,* he says. And he's laughing. Hard."

"No," Anna whispered. "You're lying!" She stood up and looked at Beverly. "Did you tell her this? Did you tell her about the skeleton? Are you two in cahoots?"

Beverly rocked back and held her palms open. "Swear to God, I did not. You mean the story where you two stole a skeleton at a party?"

"No, *Bev*. You know exactly what the fuck I'm talking about! How he rigged the skeleton to scare me when I went into the shed. Don't play dumb!"

"Honey," Beverly said with a flat affect. "You never told me anything of the sort."

Anna held her glare, then turned to Theresa, who shrugged. It was true. The only ones who knew about that booby trap in the shed were Anna and Alec.

And apparently, Graham.

Chapter 18

Anna sat back down after her accusatory outburst. She felt like a fool, on top of being a raging bitch. She shrunk in embarrassment. But she also felt detached from reality, sitting in this cold, dark room, around a table as they tried to summon the spirit of her dead husband.

Her mouth ran dry, so she asked for a sip of Bev's sarsaparilla. Beverly obliged, insisting she keep it, and stepped out of the room to get herself another.

This left Anna alone in the room with Theresa, thickening the tension with a dose of awkwardness. She thought about apologizing or making small talk when the old woman spoke first.

"It's not unusual," she said, tinkering with the alignment of her talismans. "The thought that a loved one is in the room—especially when you're freshly grieving—is very hard. I'm actually surprised you didn't storm out of here and leave."

Anna shrugged. "Bev drove, so . . ."

Theresa chuckled. "Ah. That explains it."

"I'm so sorry," Anna said, her shoulders dropping. "It's exactly what you said—it's all too much. I haven't even accepted that he's gone yet, so the thought of hearing from him is a bit of a mindfuck. I'm just surprised Bev isn't conscious of this, as a grief counselor. You know?"

"*Grief counselor?* Did Beverly get herself a new career since I spoke with her last?"

Anna frowned. "Well . . . that's how I know her, anyway. She's the counselor for our widow support group. I'm sure it's not her *career*."

"God, no," Bev said as she entered the room, sipping her fresh Sioux City Sarsaparilla bottle. "If I did that for a living, I'd kill myself. I'm not a counselor any more than you're a fighter pilot, Anna. I'm a support group *facilitator*. There's no degree or certification. Just a PowerPoint presentation, online test, and a laminated cheat sheet."

While Anna hadn't thought about Bev's qualifications before, learning this did have some effect on her trust in the elder woman's judgment. An educated and licensed counselor would be going out on a limb to drag a patient or client to a fortune teller. But a *facilitator?* Just another uneducated Jane Schmoe? Now Anna *really* felt foolish.

Once again, she felt compelled to get up and leave, but no longer out of anger. Now she just wanted to go because this was stupid. But just as before, Bev had driven, so she was stuck here.

Theresa raised her eyebrows at Anna. "Would you like to proceed? I understand if it's too soon."

This no longer felt like sorcery. It felt more like role-playing. While she wasn't up for games in her current state, it seemed more important to be a good sport rather than throwing the bullshit flag or pulling the sensitivity card.

"It's fine. Let's continue," she said.

The three of them retook their positions, forming a ring around the table with their linked hands, Theresa's both facing upward. The sorceress repeated her mantra again—which, to Anna, now held all the merit of the thoughts and prayers offered after another mass shooting.

"Hear these words, hear my cry, spirit from the other side. Come to me, I summon thee. Cross now the great divide."

Anna was happy in her aloof and detached mentality when a visceral reminder brought her back to the panic point that had sent her spiraling moments earlier.

The air chilled.

Hair stood up on her arms again. At some point since her outburst, the room had reverted to its normal temperature, without her noticing. And now, after she found the sense to dismiss this all as gobbledygook, the cold air brought her back into the fold, like a sobering bucket of ice water.

Her aloofness left the room with the heat, and then the old woman spoke.

"He's back," she said. "And—I'm sorry, but it sounds like . . . he's *laughing.*"

A shiver wiggled its way up Anna's spine. Her mind raced, once again trying to make sense of so many inputs, some of which told her the truth was fiction, and the rest told her to believe what her five senses reported. But in the end, her mind came to a stop on one single thought.

Of course he's laughing. That's my Graham.

Chapter 19

"He has a message for you," Theresa said, her brow furrowed. "And he's asking nicely that you don't interrupt him again."

Anna's hands and feet had gone cold—partly from the frigid air, and partly from anticipation and fear. Did she even want this? It didn't matter. Whether or not Graham was sitting at a phone on the other side of the invisible barrier between life and the hereafter had become, in the last few minutes, a matter of interpretation.

She wanted to break down in tears, but that would interrupt this process—whatever its output. Equal parts of her mind *wanted* to believe one thing, while the other *had* to believe the opposite. And before she could assign a belief to each side, they'd flip.

Her grip on the truth became slick.

"Graham wants to make sure you know it's him. He's asking you to say—uh . . . your *safe word?*" Theresa leaned toward Anna and whispered, "I promise this question is not mine."

Now Anna had to wonder if this was all a ruse. Were Bev and Theresa collaborating to make a viral video? In what universe would it make sense for her to divulge the safe word she had with her late husband? Besides, they'd never done any kinky sadomasochistic stuff sexually. Just as she began to say she didn't know what word he could possibly mean, Theresa closed her eyes, turned her nose up, and elaborated.

"For tickling," she said. "He wants the *tickling* safe word."

Before she could blink, two streams of tears rolled down Anna's face. It was definitely Graham. No one else knew they'd even had a safe word for their tickle fights—except maybe the boys.

Graham was relentless—in so many ways, but fallibly so in his quest for a laugh. When he and Anna decided to engage in play, it was war. He'd attack her flanks, where she was most ticklish, and she'd aim to probe his belly button or pinch his nipples—his own Achilles' heels. One night, after a tickle fight in which Graham gained the upper hand and could tickle her unabated, it became a legitimate fight. When it was over, he lay cackling on the floor as Anna clocked him in the jaw. Only then did he realize her anger was no longer playful. A lengthy discussion took place, and at the end, a safe word was established.

"Purple Skittles," Anna said, snot bubbling from one nostril. She accepted a tissue from Beverly.

Bev snorted, holding back a laugh. "I'm sorry. But I look forward to hearing the story behind this."

"So you know it's your Graham?" Theresa asked—the way a lawyer might ask for verbal confirmation from a witness on the stand. "Can you tell him you know it's him in the room with us?"

Anna looked down and sobbed, tears and snot dripping onto her lap. She couldn't fathom how this could be a scam, her imagination, or a mere illusion. He'd given her proof. She'd be a fool to ignore it. All doubt was gone. She said the only thing she could. "Yes. I know it's him."

Theresa kept her eyes squeezed shut, and delivered the next message. "He says he only has one thing to say to you. And he thinks you know what it is."

There were so many things Graham might say from the dead. *I love you. Tell the boys I love them. I miss you.* Any of those trite things would make sense. But Graham was unpredictable by nature—by his own intelligent design—and all for the sake of a laugh.

Something in the air felt different to Anna. He had to be in the room with them, and he wanted to say something she'd never expect. She felt this conviction, and knew the sensation was true. Through the moisture on her face, with her eyes shut, she beat him to the punch, replying to his message before he could send it to her. It took all her composure to say the words out loud before breaking down in an ugly cry.

"I forgive you."

Chapter 20

After Anna professed her mercy to Graham, the tone of the séance changed. She broke down into a pile, sobbing into her arms on the table until it became apparent to Bev and Theresa that she could do this indefinitely. Theresa started turning lights back on, mumbling about the time.

Bev pulled Theresa away to negotiate payment for this experience, given that there had been minimal communication with the *other side*. At the end of that conversation, they secretly agreed on a price. Once Anna regained her composure, Theresa addressed her.

"I realize you may not have gotten everything you wanted out of this experience, whatever that might be. I'll only charge you fifty bucks, which is a quarter of the usual amount for these services. If you'd like to come back, my rates are very reasonable, whatever service you want. I only have to charge enough to keep the lights on in this place, and that ain't much since I sleep most of the days."

Anna nodded absently. "Thanks. I'll think about it. Do you take Venmo? CashApp?"

The elder's wrinkled face creased harder. "Pardon?"

"Zelle, maybe? How should I pay you?"

Theresa chortled. "Money! Dollar bills." She glanced at Bev. "What is this world coming to? Does the American dollar exist anymore?"

Anna fumbled through her purse, eventually finding a twenty. She handed it to Theresa and looked at Bev. "Do you carry cash? Can you spot me thirty?"

Bev nodded, then flashed a look at Theresa. "Just put it on my tab, friend. Include a fair tip."

Theresa scoffed at her friend, then regarded Anna. "When you come back, don't bring *this one* with you every time," Theresa said, thumbing toward Beverly. "I don't need her drinking all my sarsaparilla!"

The two women riffed while Anna tuned them out. She stared out one of the filmy windows at the open sky, wondering where it ended. Where this plane of existence ended, and the next one began.

Saying goodbye to Theresa and leaving the rural property was a blur. By the time Anna pulled herself out of the shock of contacting Graham, she and Beverly were in the Buick, easing into the Minneapolis suburbs, zoning out to the one-note hum of the big car's big engine.

Bev broke the silence. "Oh—Theresa threw in a little something extra that she wanted you to take home. She said it's been waiting for its rightful owner."

"Oh, God. I'm not sure I can handle more than I already got."

Beverly fished around behind her seat, feeling for something inside her handbag. After a couple of swerves left of center, she held up a fancy-looking bottle of red wine. "She said Graham picked it out himself."

"Bullshit," Anna said, taking the bottle and studying it. It was a 1976 pinot noir—bottled in Ontario, Canada. She gasped.

"I don't understand how you can be such a doubting Thomas after what just happened. Theresa is legit." Bev looked over at Anna, who'd gone pale. "You okay? You look like you've seen a ghost! Er . . . sorry, you know what I mean."

Anna stared at the label. "Graham was born in 1976. In Ontario. And that's when this wine was bottled. In Ontario." She glanced up at Bev with moisture in her eyes.

Bev turned back to the road. "Like I said. Theresa is legit. Maybe if you have a glass, you'll be sharing it with him. I dunno. All I know is she gave it to you for some reason, and you can't make this stuff up. You think she's waiting around for someone to show up whose late husband was born that year? *And* in Canada? Even if she did, how did she have the bottle ready? She didn't go to a wine cellar or anything. It was sitting there on the rack."

It was as if Beverly had verbalized Anna's swirling thoughts. It couldn't be a coincidence. If anything, it was all a setup—but why? She'd never told Bev or Theresa any of those details about Graham. And it sure as shit wasn't commonplace for a couple to have a safe word specifically for tickle fights.

There was truth to this. It was undeniable.

They pulled into the parking lot of the shopping center where Anna had parked her car. It was still packed with the cars of after-dark consumers. Anna hated this time of year. The early sunset and cold that came with it felt lifeless and hopeless. And now, compounded by the hole in her life, the darkness was unbearable.

Bev parked behind Anna's car. "You sure you're good to drive?"

Anna glanced down at the bottle of wine, then back at Bev. "What? I haven't been drinking."

"I know, but . . . still. I can drop you off at home if you want."

"Thanks—but I'm fine. I'll be alright." Anna wasn't certain of this, but she *was* positive she didn't want Beverly to know where she lived. Not because she thought Bev would ever break into her house and set up pranks that could be credited to Graham, but because she needed to eliminate that as a possibility—for her own sanity.

"Call me if you feel like you're losing it, okay? I don't do shit these days, so you won't be an inconvenience to anything but my stupid phone games or whatever trashy novel I'm reading. I mean it."

"Will do," Anna said, knowing there was no way. She needed to be alone to make sense of this. And it might be a while.

Because it made zero sense.

Chapter 21

Anna arrived home and collapsed on the couch, still clutching the bottle of aged wine. She stared at the ceiling and stroked the greying blond hair on her head with her free hand, contemplating pulling it all out.

Her brain couldn't compute what she'd experienced. She'd delved into sorcery to contact her dead love, and almost certainly succeeded. The medium through which he spoke to her could not have been fabricating the communication—Theresa had relayed messages only she and Graham would understand. Even now, as she lay staring at the popcorn ceiling that Graham had pledged for years he'd remove, Anna held a bottle of wine that might've been born within moments of him, and only a short drive away.

Nothing in the logic that Anna adhered to could solve this equation. She drew her phone from her pocket and unlocked it, navigating to the web page she'd become addicted to. After a few cycles from start to finish, she noticed a new video in the *similar content* section. The thumbnail image showed a skyscraper under construction, from the street-level vantage point.

Anna swallowed hard. There was no way she could keep herself from clicking. So she clicked.

With the same ritualistic masochism she practiced on a regular basis, Anna watched Graham's flailing body plummet to the sidewalk with a loud clap. His buttercup-yellow hard hat broke in two, the fragments flying in opposite directions. Her husband's body—the same one she would never spoon ever again—bounced, stalling in midair, limp and lifeless. Bystanders screamed or shouted in shock, but the videographer kept the lens trained on Graham's empty vessel as a pool of crimson spread around him.

When it ended, that circular arrow sat there, taunting her. *Play it again*, it begged. And of course, she did. She always would.

With each replay, new morbid details came to her attention. Someone behind the camera snickered when his body bounced, as if it were slapstick comedy. Another loudmouthed witness yelled for someone to call the coroner. People who noticed the person recording the incident crowded in the frame, eager to get their seconds of fame for this inevitably immortal video.

To them it was a spectacle. For her, it was the end of the world as she knew it.

Anna sat up and looked at the clock, realizing she'd been viewing her husband's death footage for two hours. Worse yet, she was no closer to understanding any of this than she'd been when she walked through the front door.

"What the hell," she muttered as she trudged through the living room and into the kitchenette area. With a lackadaisical plop, she set the wine bottle on the dining table and retrieved a wine glass from the cupboard. Maybe a glass or two would loosen her up to possibilities her sober mind refused to entertain.

As Anna set the glass down on the table, she contemplated filling it with the cheap chardonnay chilling in the fridge. If she needed to take the edge off, that'd do just fine. But she looked over at the old bottle of wine and knew, beyond any doubt, that she needed to at least taste it.

It took a few minutes to locate a corkscrew, since her typical wine containers were equipped with twist-off caps. Once she found it, she pulled the cork from the old bottle. Anna was no wine connoisseur, but the unleashed aroma of the fermented grape juice hit her hard in the nose. It smelled familiar, the way the smell of a leaf pile took her back to childhood, but she couldn't place it. Maybe it was the musk notes, or the richness of age, but the scent tantalized her.

She poured the glass half full, to the widest part of the bowl, and swirled it the way she'd seen snobby people do on TV. And just as they did, she poked her nose inside the glass, like an ill-fitting oxygen mask, and sniffed the flavors of what she knew must be a fine wine.

This was why she could never be a class better than her own. It smelled like red wine. She couldn't identify the character of it, or describe it poetically. All the smell did was make her want to drink it.

Like the novice she was, Anna took a healthy sip, shrugged, then followed up by drinking half of the glass's contents. It had a bite to it, like it had more alcohol than anything she'd find at the grocery store—but it otherwise failed to impress her.

She tilted the bottle, and the fine print at the bottom of the label came into focus. Not only had this bottle of wine been born in 1976 —the year of Graham's birth—and bottled in Ontario—Graham's province of birth. No—the gold print on the off-white background proclaimed that the grapes of this wine had been stomped, fermented, and bottled in the city of Thunder Bay.

Graham's very birthplace.

What the fuck.

Anna brought the bottle with her as she took a seat at the dinette and tried to digest what she'd experienced at Theresa's house. No matter how many holes she tried to poke in the mystical explanations, she came up empty. And regardless of any conspiracy between Bev and Theresa she hypothesized, it wouldn't add up.

Two and a half-overfilled glasses deep, Anna turned to go to the bathroom—she hadn't relieved herself since before they ventured to Theresa's hocus-pocus haven. As she sat on the john and peed, part of her expected the door to fly open, the way it would when Graham was feeling cheeky. He'd always be ready to prank her or the boys, but sometimes he'd breach the line between good humor and privacy invasion.

When he made the decision to encroach in such a way, it was implied that he thought it was worth it. Yes, he'd get yelled at. Maybe even threatened with weapons of opportunity. But in Graham's weird mind, it was an acceptable risk—because it was certain to be funny enough. To himself, at least.

He had ninja-like abilities. Not only could Graham creep quietly across a creaky floor to pounce on his prey—that was beginner-level skill—he could unlock a door from outside the room without giving himself away. He was a *master*. He'd twist the doorknob with a stealth the Department of Defense could've exploited as a weapon of war.

But Graham had never employed his powers for material gain. There was a much more valuable end to his means. He'd kick open the bathroom door, timed in such a way that his mark was in mid-squeeze. They'd tense up and fire the turd out with explosive force. The audible plop of the shit hitting the water was the coup de grâce —whatever the consequences, hearing that telltale splash, accompanied by a shriek of terror, was the pinnacle of success for the operation.

So now, as Anna sat on the commode, her classically conditioned response was to watch the doorknob and the shadow beneath the doorjamb to verify her safety from such an attack—despite knowing she was alone.

Or was she?

In accordance with all logic and reason, Graham's ghost didn't kick the bathroom door open to literally scare the shit out of Anna. But she urinated long enough to realize how long she'd neglected her basic needs. She hadn't eaten since before Bev picked her up for the trip to Theresa's. Upon standing, the buzz of the rich wine struck her, making her voyage down the stairs precarious. She staggered back into the kitchen and poked her head into the pantry, and then the refrigerator.

All the Top Ramen packets were gone from the pantry, and pizza from almost a week ago sat in the fridge, but Anna wasn't drunk enough to call that sustenance. Rather than seeking a better dinner, she decided to pour another glass of wine from 1976 and consider her options. Or at least become intoxicated enough to lower her standards.

When she turned from the fridge toward the table to pseudo-savor another healthy glass of wine, Anna froze. There it was, looking back at her from its place on the dinette table.

A second glass of red wine.

Chapter 22

Anna was strangely relieved when she had no choice but to accept that Graham's ghost was in the room with her. The debate in her mind was over, and logic had lost. Agnosticism would no longer be an option. She'd have to grieve alone. No one would believe her, except Bev and Theresa, leaving her trust with only dabblers in the occult.

Life as she understood it was over.

Before she could decide how to react—to call Bev, or Alec, or simply run out of the house screaming for help—the room fell darker, until she was looking through a pinhole of light at the two glasses full of mahogany wine. As Anna fell backward, aware she was losing consciousness, a familiar sound confirmed that fainting was the appropriate response.

Graham laughing.

He had an unmistakable giggle. Though his voice was baritone, his laugh was high-pitched and somewhat maniacal. And it intensified exponentially, as if the sound of his own laughter was the funniest thing he'd ever heard.

Anna had never before passed out, so it took her the better part of a minute to realize what'd happened—to remember where she'd 'left off' in consciousness and regain her grasp on reality. She'd had intense, vivid dreams while she was out, but couldn't recall a single detail from them now. But as the facts reemerged in her brain, she remembered that reality was less comprehensible than her wildest fantasies.

It was as if she were floating away from shore, beyond the point where her feet could touch the bottom. The current was too strong to swim against without exhausting herself. Her only choice was to drift out to sea and hope some passing watercraft found her before she succumbed to the ocean.

Was this what crazy felt like?

It was a fair question. Anna sat up and looked at the dinette table to see two wine glasses, both filled to the pour line—a reasonable spot just above the fat part of the bowl, rather than near the rim, where Anna had been filling hers.

Nothing made sense. She glanced at the oven clock. 12:33 a.m.— too late to call anyone. Slowly, Anna got in position to stand up, taking care not to bring on another headrush. As she stood, she stared at the glasses.

What now? Should she have a seat and drink her wine, assuming her dead soulmate sat in the other chair, invisibly doing the same in some other dimension?

Would that make anything better?

No. Graham died because of his own foolishness, leaving her to cope alone in this empty nest. He'd been selfish, and now she had to suffer the consequences of his actions—as did their sons. While she missed and loved him more in death than she'd ever appreciated him in life, she resented his lack of consideration for anyone but himself— for the sake of his own amusement.

The loss was bad enough. But now he had the nerve to haunt her, continuing his mischief as though nothing had changed when he died. Graham always tried to defuse tense situations with a dose of lightheartedness, but to the point of denial. He'd laugh at a funeral, not as a counterintuitive way to cope with grief, but to break the heavy tension. Not his best quality.

Anna knew that, in his own mind, Graham only wanted to make any situation better for everyone involved. But he lacked consideration for the impact his actions would have on others. Rather than change at all, or examine why he behaved that way, he doubled down. *Graham gonna be Graham*, he'd say with that giggle. It was bullshit. Immature, narcissistic bullshit.

Everyone had to clean up his messes but him.

Anna's knees started to ache. She looked at the oven clock again: 1:44 a.m. She'd been standing in the middle of her kitchen—seething as she stared at the wine glasses—for over an hour.

It was time to act. She couldn't very well kick back, have one more glass of wine with her husband's ghost, and then turn in for the night. In the back of her mind, Anna knew she was at a crossroads. What she did at this juncture would set the course for the rest of her life—a part of her existence that wouldn't include Graham, no matter what she decided.

She marched to the table and snatched up one of the glasses, tilted her head back, and poured the entire serving into her gaping mouth. Wine spilled as she tried to gulp it all down, splashing onto her clothes and the linoleum floor.

"You're dead!" she shouted, glaring at the empty chair across the table. "*Dead!* Do you even understand that? And you can't drink wine. Only *I* can! Because *I* am alive! Here, by myself, while you're still playing your stupid jokes on me. But you're *dead*. You understand? *Dead!*"

Anna picked up the second glass and gave it the same treatment, with even less of the wine making it into her mouth. Her face twisted in a silent cry, then she hurled the glass at the empty chair where Graham presumably sat.

It shattered, the clinks in some way feeding Anna's rage. She grabbed the other glass and did the same. With no more glass to break, she flipped the dinette table over and screamed at the chair until her lungs went empty.

"I lied to you, Graham. I *don't* forgive you! Do you understand me? You left me! You left *us*. All for what, a joke? For some internet fame? To amuse your work buddies? Was it worth it, Graham? You dumb, selfish asshole! Huh? *Was it?*"

She picked up the wooden chair where she imagined he sat and hurled it across the kitchen. Its legs splintered as it slammed against the sturdy cabinets. The destruction set off something inside her—a conduit for all her rage at death and the man who brought it upon himself. She gripped one of the broken legs and flung it blindly. Before she could see where it went, the sound of shattering glass indicated she'd broken the kitchen window. Cold air rushed in, scolding her for her recklessness.

Another terrible mess she had no idea how to clean up. At least this time it was her own fault.

This bout of exertion sapped the last bit of energy keeping Anna functional. She collapsed cross-legged on the floor, then soon lay back, weeping until tears sealed her eyes for the night.

Chapter 23

A knock at the door awoke Anna. Judging by the amount of sunlight in the room, it had to be early morning. The raps on the door came in quick succession, and firmly—like the summons of authority. When she stood, her balance was off, reminding her how drunk she'd gotten the night before.

With the help of the sofa arm and end table, she managed to reach the front door. Before opening it, she looked down at herself. Her grey shirt was splashed with cerise stains, and for some reason her hands had trails of dried blood on them. It seemed wise not to answer the door, until another barrage of aggressive knocks resounded inches from her sensitive ears. She opened it.

A police officer waited, his posture foreboding but his face kind. He said something into the radio mic on his shoulder before greeting Anna. "Good morning, ma'am. Everything okay here?"

Anna rubbed her forehead. "Yeah—I'm good. Everything's fine. Just had a few last night. Why do you ask?"

"We got a request called in for a welfare check," he said, flipping through his notepad. "Apparently, last night there was some shouting and glass breaking? And this morning, we're told all the lights were still on, so concerned neighbors asked us to check on you."

"Oh, okay. Well, I'm fine. Thanks for checking on me." Anna nodded and began to close the door.

"If you don't mind, can I ask you a couple questions?" the officer said. "And I assure you, you're not in trouble or anything. No crime has been committed. We just have to make sure we complete our investigation. Is that fair?"

Anna massaged her temples, looking downward to avoid the harsh sunlight. "Uh—sure, I guess that's okay."

The cop took on a Boy Scout persona. "Mind if I come in and sit? It's easier to write things down if I'm sitting."

She looked behind her to see how much of the mess in her house would be visible if he sat on the couch. "No, sure. Of course. Come on in, sir."

The officer stepped in as Anna pulled the door open wider. He took a glimpse of everything in sight. "No need to call me sir. Name's Joe Steffen. Please, call me Joe."

"Okay. Have a seat wherever, Joe. Can I offer you something to drink?"

He flipped his notepad to a blank page. "No, but thank you. Feel free to sit as well."

Anna nodded. She tried to plant herself in the love seat but landed her butt on its arm. Snorting a laugh, she tried to play it off then slid down into the seat. "So, I'm sorry if I'm a little sloppy, but I had some wine last night, and it was—well, it was a bit stronger than I thought. So I might still be drunk. So, uh . . . you know, can you please write that down? I don't think I'm in a good state to be answering questions for cops, is all."

Joe waved, pen in hand. "Oh, don't worry. I'm only here to assist. But I will document everything you tell me, for sure. First, can you explain why the neighbors might've heard shouting from this residence last night? Were you alone?"

She snickered before answering. "I was. I was alone."

He nodded slowly. "So, the shouting . . . were you on the phone, maybe?"

"No, I wasn't on the phone."

Joe froze, his eyes darting around. He wrote something down. "I see. Okay, well—let's move on from that. What about the sounds of breaking glass? Does that have anything to do with the cuts on your hands? I see you lost a bit of blood there."

Anna glanced down at her arms, trying to appear casual. But the sight of blood trails along her forearms gave her some alarm. She tried to laugh it off, but it came out as a whimpering cry. Now it was clear she was going through something, so she took a deep breath and prepared to tell the best version of the truth she could put together.

"So, full disclosure or whatever . . . my husband recently died."

"Oh, I'm so sorry to hear that."

"Right—so, but . . . I'm just having a really hard time dealing with it, because weird things have been happening around here lately, and I think he might be haunting me." She let out a nervous laugh. "I know that sounds ridiculous, and I get it—believe me, I do. But . . . last night, I hit a breaking point. *Literally.* I broke a couple wine glasses. And it seems I got a few cuts in the process."

The officer focused on his notepad as he jotted down a lengthy entry. "Okay, then. I can understand what you're probably going through. If you don't mind, can I ask if you've sought out any grief counseling since your husband's death?"

"I have, yes."

"Oh, excellent! That's the first step in a situation like yours. A lot of people are afraid to ask for help. Do you mind if I ask why you think your late husband is haunting you?"

Officer Steffen probed for enough details that he expressed obvious concern for her mental health. Anna admitted that the facilitator of her widow support group had taken her to a spiritual medium, who'd unequivocally put her in contact with Graham, who now played pranks on her from beyond the realm of the living. It sounded crazy, but that's what'd happened.

She rambled like a drunkard on the street.

As silly as the cop might think it was, Anna was telling the truth as she perceived it. And it felt right. Joe Steffen was so empathetic and nonjudgmental that she divulged her deepest resentments toward Graham, breaking down at several points. She led him to the kitchen and re-enacted the scene from the night before, explaining how it was most certainly Graham sitting in that seat. Whether or not the wine glasses did him any damage, she wasn't sure, but there was no doubt in her mind he'd been sitting there when she threw them at him.

It wasn't until Officer Joe Steffen excused himself to consult with his supervisor out front—where another police cruiser sat, ensconced by a small audience of nosy neighbors—that Anna wondered at what point she'd said too much.

Because by then, she had zero doubt she'd said too much.

Chapter 24

J oe Steffen brought Anna into the station with her consent, though she couldn't recall when or why she'd agreed—this cop had a velvet tongue, it seemed. She wanted no part in any services or further investigations, but his friendly demeanor and Howdy-Doody face had lured her into a slow walk to his car, during which they both ignored the noise around them.

She'd hesitated to sit in the passenger seat of his cruiser until the officer promised to stop at McDonald's for a Sausage McMuffin with egg. After all, she had also confessed to him that she was famished.

As Anna scarfed down her breakfast sandwich, she realized something in her destiny had shifted. Only then did she reconsider the last words she'd directed at Graham—that he was unforgiven. The intimacy of that moment was raw, and her emotions were justified. But still, she loved him. He was her person, and she his. Partners in crime. Sometimes literally.

Even in death, their bond was sacred. Yet here Anna was in a cop car, on her way to the station to put Graham on paper for reaching out to her from the afterlife.

She was snitching.

It hit her in waves, as though the universe knew she couldn't take it all in at one time. But it was the truth.

Sure, Graham was an immature asshole and mistakenly left his loving family for the sake of a gag. And sure, he'd capitalized on some inside jokes with his favorite person—from the dead—to remind her he was still there. To get a laugh, even if it was only for him.

Because what better reminder could he give her?

He'd spoken to her in the language he knew best. All along, through the years of torment and borderline abuse, in the post-traumatic stress she might never recover from, he'd spoken his native love tongue to say the most important thing he could communicate to her.

I love you.

So little of that mattered now, as Anna sat in a chair at Officer Steffen's desk. He offered reassurances that nothing terrible would happen as a result of her confessions while he multitasked through his emails and some other work applications. She could tell she was being held until someone else could take on the workload she'd created by telling this lawman her truth.

While she waited, images of Graham's body bouncing off the concrete flashed in her mind. He'd been alive for 120 feet as he fell, and forty-two years before that. With that jarring smack, space and time were distorted in a way that rendered Anna's world obsolete. Life with a soulmate would be a thing of the past. The thought of what would replace it made her ill.

Chunks of sausage patty, English muffin, and egg tumbled in her stomach, as if to send her a signal. But it was too late. The damage was already done.

A plump woman with an iPad, a smile, and an I-won't-hurt-you posture pulled a chair in front of Anna and sat. This manifested only one loud thought.

What the fuck have I done?

Anna quickly learned that trying to prove one's sanity was a lot like escaping quicksand: the harder she fought, the worse her chances of success.

She spent what felt like hours answering the woman's strangely worded and open-ended questions with the sole objective of demonstrating the soundness of her mind. When the woman stopped typing and simply nodded at Anna with a face bent in sympathy, she knew she was sinking deeper.

It was hard to explain what'd happened in the last few days without coming off as crazy. No matter how many times she re-explained the events leading up to her so-called 'self-harm incident' with a factual tone, the story had to end with her throwing wine glasses at the empty chair where her deceased husband's ghost was sitting.

After a while, she began to ask the question herself.

Am I going insane?

It wasn't easy to answer. Maybe she *hadn't* been crazy until Graham started playing his pranks from the other side. So, regardless of whether things had happened as she believed, the end result was Anna losing touch with reality. If that wasn't the case, she could only wonder how much of what she'd experienced had been real, and how much was a result of her psychosis.

Only then did Anna wonder if she'd ever go home again.

Chapter 25

The woman—Richelle, per the badge clipped to her breast pocket—had a soothing demeanor. Her raspy voice comforted Anna, even as it fired probing questions about the last few weeks.

Richelle escorted Anna to a quiet room with plush chairs and a water cooler. She shared her own experience after her brother was murdered, encountering strange coincidences for months that made her certain he was watching over her. Her eyes pooled with tears, sealing Anna's belief that her sympathy was genuine.

A potent combination of trust and fatigue rendered Anna vulnerable enough to tell Richelle some of the more intricate details of her hauntings. The woman stopped jotting things down and laughed with Anna through all the absurdity she'd struggled to make sense of. It was only when she revealed how many times and how often she watched the video of Graham's death that Richelle's demeanor shifted.

"Anna, that's not at all the appropriate way to process the trauma of seeing that horrible event. All you're doing is distancing yourself from his humanity. You're dissociating."

"I'm fine. Really—it bothers me still. I just watch it to help bring the feelings out."

Richelle shook her head as she resumed taking notes. "You did say you've been somnambulating, did you not? Sleepwalking?"

"I . . . did I say that? I don't think so."

"You did."

This brought Anna to a state of alarm, triggering a tidbit in her memory from a YouTuber she followed—a former attorney who posted tips on how to behave during interactions with the police. He demonstrated the use of numerous tactics and terminology in action with real cops, and they always worked. Like magic spells. One of the key phrases he urged his followers to employ came back to her now.

"Tell me this, Richelle. Am I being detained? Or am I free to go?" Anna sat back and crossed her arms, as though she'd just declared checkmate. In the YouTube videos, the only answer to that question was exactly what she wanted—and expected—to hear.

"As of right now, yes. You're being detained for your own safety."

Fuck. Didn't see that coming.

Richelle continued, "But that doesn't mean you're under arrest, or being charged with a crime, alright? This is a very normal process when we encounter someone who may be a danger to themselves."

Anna sat forward. "A danger to myself? The only danger is what's gonna happen when I finally get out of here and talk to a lawyer! Matter of fact, do I not get a phone call? I want to talk to a lawyer. I'm lawyering up."

"That's not necessary, Anna. You can make as many phone calls as you like."

It'd been a trap, all along. Her quickening pulse throbbed in her temples. She trembled with adrenaline as she stood. Richelle started to reach out to her, triggering a flight response. Anna yanked the door open and sprinted down the hall, colliding with an officer and knocking him down.

Instantly, several officers swarmed to restrain the belligerent detainee. One of them grabbed both of Anna's arms and pulled them behind her back to keep her from swinging at any of them.

Now disarmed—literally—Anna went into a panicked rage, screaming at the cops to keep their hands off her. Officer Steffen appeared and tried to approach her from the front to calm her down. In response, Anna swung her legs up and kicked a heel at Joe Steffen's face. It landed cleanly. His nose exploded blood across his face. He fell to the floor, stunned and bleeding profusely onto the linoleum.

That afternoon, Anna found herself in jail—under arrest and charged with aggravated battery and assault against a law enforcement officer. As she'd sworn to Richelle she would, she lawyered up. It took her a full two hours to provide the backstory to her attorney, who promptly recommended she plead not guilty by reason of insanity.

Although Anna swore to her lawyer that she was of sound mind, he warned her only other option would be to plead guilty or no contest, either of which meant substantial jail time. A not guilty plea was legal suicide, given that her crimes were committed in the presence of dozens of law enforcement officers. The court would have little sympathy for the circumstances unless her plea necessitated it.

Early the next morning, Anna's attorney sat beside her while the prosecutor read the terms of the plea agreement out loud and showed her where to initial and sign. Before leaving, the lawyer assured her this was the best outcome she could've hoped for. All she could do was nod and thank him for his services.

The quicksand had won. Anna was in over her head, and there would be no escape.

Chapter 26

A week after her arrest, Anna was released from jail and transferred to Hillandale Inpatient Mental Hospital for evaluation and ongoing treatment. The plea deal required that she be committed to the facility for no less than three months, and thereafter until she was discharged as fully rehabilitated.

While this interrupted her once normal life, Anna encountered few disruptions. Work put her on medical leave, and Alec took over her finances, making sure the bills got paid. He'd tried to find her a good attorney during the court proceedings, but Anna relented. A stay in a mental hospital wasn't a punishment, the way her life was going.

Bev tried to contact her numerous times, but Anna had told her therapy team about the séance, so they made sure to put Bev on the blacklist. It was thoughtful of her to be concerned about Anna—but also a little strange. Maybe she needed to collect her thirty dollars.

The Hillandale staff was kind to Anna, and she made friends with doctors, administrators, and fellow patients alike. For the first couple of weeks, no one knew the series of events that landed her there besides her designated psychologist and a schizophrenic patient named Corrina, who became her confidante.

This didn't mean no one knew why she was there. Her dossier—which was available to all staff—indicated that she believed her deceased husband had haunted her. While many patients there tended to be combative, irrational, unpredictable, or any combination of these, Anna had a reputation for being pleasant and seemingly normal—like someone who didn't belong in an inpatient facility.

One particular nurse practitioner had befriended Anna and got to know her better than anyone else there. Nurse Darcy had little professional need to interact with Anna, but the two of them spoke whenever they crossed paths, as though they were old friends.

Darcy and Anna were roughly the same age, and they shared a sense of humor. At one point, Anna felt confident they could launch a successful podcast with their riffing. Darcy trusted Anna with secrets from her own life—such as her disdain for the facility's administration, and for-profit mental hospitals in general—without ever asking Anna for a confession in kind. But Anna volunteered to tell her stories, many of which involved Graham and his shenanigans.

After her ordeal at the police station, Anna tried to keep her mouth shut about what she'd experienced with Graham's ghost. She knew her freedom hinged on reconnecting with reality, which didn't align with sticking to her supernatural story. *Her* truth could never be *the* truth.

She'd tell them whatever they needed to hear.

Nevertheless, Anna struggled to keep her story straight during her rigorous therapy schedule. Group sessions, individual sessions with her therapist, and periodic check-ins with senior doctors were a heavy burden of lies to tell.

Her psychiatrist either saw through the lies, or decided to prescribe medication regardless of the truth. Anna met with him three times a week to evaluate the efficacy of the drugs he'd prescribed. Each time, she reported no noticeable difference. Her understanding of reality was rock-solid. Two weeks in, he had her on a regimen of Seroquel—an antipsychotic.

One of the most prevalent side effects of this drug was drowsiness. On its face, this was harmless; but Anna had a hard time remembering the right things to say when sleepy. It also caused her naps to become more frequent, which in turn made her sleepwalking episodes more frequent. This led to an increase in the dosage that left Anna wondering where the line between dream and reality was.

Only Nurse Darcy ever got the unfiltered scoop from Anna. And in turn, she divulged some of the closely guarded politics of the Hillandale staff. The Medical Director for inpatient services, Dr. Pete Steele, was a tyrant.

"He comes across like a nice guy, but he's really a piece of shit," Darcy told Anna at a communal new year's party. She slurped a cube of Jell-O off her spoon and squished it around her mouth. "If I'm a bad person, I'll see his face when I die. Because that son of a bitch belongs in hell."

Anna snickered as she savored her apple pie. "That bad, huh?"

"Oh, worse. *Much* worse. Think if Hitler ran a mental institution."

"Hitler was pretty fucking horrible as it was," Anna said. "He ruled over a whole continent, committed genocide—you know, that whole thing."

Darcy stabbed her own apple pie slice. "Sure, but at least he liked dogs. Did you know that? He was a dog person. And he liked art. But *this* motherfucker, God damn. You know Steele once informed us that we'd all have to take salary cuts to avoid layoffs? He acted all somber, like he honestly didn't want to put anyone out of a job. But in the same announcement, he told us it *could* be avoided if there was a consensus among the staff as to who should be let go. He said he needed two positions eliminated to avoid the pay cuts and then disappeared into his office. I couldn't see his face, but I swear to God the motherfucker was smiling. Like some kind of survivor reality show, we had to decide whether to vote two of us off or let him slash all our paychecks."

"Damn. That's pretty cold."

"Just like his fucking heart," Nurse Darcy said, glaring at him from across the cafeteria. "I think I'd prefer Hitler."

Anna waited a moment. "So . . . what'd you guys decide?"

"We lost some good professionals. All because of petty drama. We turned on each other, just like Steele wanted. He acted like it was great news because no one had to take a pay cut, but I know he was truly happy people got laid off. He got his rocks off because we betrayed each other."

"Wow."

Darcy chomped on her bite of pie. "*Wow* is right. I only hope I live long enough to watch that old bastard take his last breath."

"Sounds like you're not his biggest fan," Anna said with a laugh.

"For sure," Darcy said. "But I'm positive the psychs hate him even more than I do."

The *psychs* were a crew of psychologists and psychiatrists who managed the ongoing therapy and medication for the patients at Hillandale. Anna had noticed how they all seemed disgruntled, but chalked it up to the pains of making progress with the criminally insane.

"Really? Like who?"

Darcy snorted. "All of 'em. And I'm pretty sure he hates them just as much. In fact, I'm probably the only one around here he trusts."

"You do come off as trustworthy," Anna said, pointing at Darcy with her fork. "Something in your face—or maybe your demeanor. I trusted you right away."

"Oh, stop," Darcy said, flapping her hand at Anna.

It was the truth. Coming into the facility, Anna trusted no one. Her candor had led to Officer Steffen and Richelle (and in turn, her own attorney) putting her in this place. She hadn't been honest with anyone since—not until she met Nurse Darcy. Shortly after they met,

Anna divulged more to her than she ever would to her therapists. She couldn't sit alone with the grief she felt, because her mind couldn't process it. Even Beverly had understood that.

The building that'd become Anna's home was full of mental health professionals and drugs, but her only source of sanity was a nurse who seemed to hate the place as much as she did.

Chapter 27

One night, months into Anna's residence at Hillandale, an orderly on break went to retrieve a paper plate to microwave a French bread pizza. When he did, a throng of ping-pong balls washed over him and onto the tile floor, bouncing en masse for a duration that drew the attention of everyone on duty, including the shift supervisor.

No one ever claimed responsibility for the prank.

Not long after that incident, the shift supervisor was summoned when a series of loud popping sounds came from Anna's room. The supervisor and two nurses entered to find Anna sitting on the toilet, embarrassed and hiding herself. She stood and lifted the toilet seat to show the staff the source of the noise.

Taped to the bottom of the seat were a half dozen Pop-Its, all expended.

Anna insisted she had no idea where they'd come from, or who'd taped them to the seat. Although there was no evidence to back it up, the running theory was that Anna found a way to smuggle in some snap bang poppers and played the prank on herself.

This speculation lost some merit when a prank occurred while

Anna was nowhere near the scene of the supposed crime. She was eating breakfast with Corinna and the resident psychiatrist when the attending supervisor approached their table.

"Who put pieces of sticky notes on the bottom of everyone's mouses?" Dr. Steele said, hands on his hips. He held up a finger with a tiny pink square of paper stuck to its tip. "Literally every computer has these on the light sensor so that the mouse doesn't work. No one's in trouble, okay? But I need to know who did this, so I can address it one-on-one. The pranks are getting out of hand, guys. We have work to do."

Along with everyone else in the cafeteria, Anna shrugged. "I've been out here all morning," she said, fighting laughter. "Ask anyone."

Soon after that, someone discovered salt in the sugar container—by pouring it into their coffee, which was ruined before violating the poor sap's palate. Another fruitless investigation ensued. A few Pop-Its went off on the bottom of a random patient's toilet seat. Again, no culprit was identified.

Then, in front of nearly everyone, Dr. Steele strode with purpose, as he usually did, into the open doorway to his office. But as he breached the threshold, his upper body snapped back, and he found himself swimming in clear plastic wrap.

Someone had booby-trapped his doorway.

Anna laughed, but held her hands up to signify her innocence. Furthermore, she had a rock-solid alibi. Dr. Steele had left his office while Anna was in a session with her psychologist, Dr. Wolfe, and she went straight from there to the cafeteria. Dr. Wolfe walked with her the entire way, and she corroborated this when Dr. Steele leveled accusations directly against Anna. There was absolutely no way Anna could have done it.

When the investigation reached yet another impasse, Dr. Steele exercised his authority to seize all the closed-circuit surveillance recordings. There were twelve cameras on each floor, and two floors dedicated to secure outpatient services, which meant thousands of hours of footage to review, covering just the two days before the incident.

Three days after launching the unofficial investigation, Dr. Steele sat before the glow of his three monitors when he caught sight of what he'd set out to find: unequivocal evidence of the true culprit. He should've shouted, or otherwise exclaimed his vindication. But all he could do was cover his mouth, staring at the still shot on the screen, and whisper to himself.

"Unbelievable."

Acknowledgments

Despite the brevity of this story, it took a village to raise it from rough draft to completed novella. If I forget anyone, I blame my diminishing faculties. What day is it? I'd like to buy a vowel!

First, I must thank my forever-editor, Alex Thieme, for being much more than that. Alex also sees my raw products before anyone else does and gives me an honest but invaluable assessment, the way a proctologist might do (but it's wayyyyy less uncomfortable). She distilled feedback from beta readers (of which she was one), helped me find the right talent to perpetuate this indie author adventure, artfully reassured me I'm a good writer, and at every turn reminded me that I'm doing what I was born to do. Also, she designed my cover and consistently made me laugh in an endeavor that brings most authors to tears. Alex is fucking gold. Stay away, she's mine.

My favorite cousin, Darcy Lindner (sorry, other cousins), not only helped me shape this silly story, but also has an unspoken way of telling me when I'm on the right track with every project. Her feedback can at times be . . . direct, but I'd expect nothing less from Aunty Mo's daughter. I know it comes from nothing but love.

Cary Bright, wife-of-my-high-school-buddy-but-also-a-person-I-always-got-along-with-independently, provided her insight for this story as well. In addition to the preceding lengthy title, Cary is a fellow self-published author. If poetry is your jam, please check out Beestings and Afterthoughts—Musings around Removing the Stinger.

Upwork, the greatest resource for freelance talent in the history of mankind, made not only this publication possible, but my debut novel, The One and Only Fat Chance. I was able to systematically whittle a robust candidate pool down to the best available for beta readers, web designers, formatters, cover designers, and so forth. Also, I own stock in Upwork, so you should give Upwork money, however you're able to. I think this qualifies as a disclosure (read it and weep, SEC).

To expound on said talent, I want to give a shout out to Rachel Froelich, Laura Anne Fitzgerald, and Catherine Tillotson for providing me valuable feedback on the refined draft of this story. I hope each of you reads the final version and sees the impact you had on it. Special thanks to Jennifer Meller for working down to the wire because of my poor planning (and another thank you to Alex for the same reason).

Kate Norwalk, the love of my life and the saint who not only endures my Graham-like qualities but embraces them, inspired this story. She's so much a part of who I am now that I can promise that she'll inspire many more stories to come. Kate's my person, and I truly hope I never get her institutionalized. But if I do . . . she knew what she was getting herself into from Day One.

I don't talk about my day job with my kids, because it's boring. Meaningless and stupid, albeit lucrative. But I have to thank them for always listening to my silly story ideas and letting me know how this sordid new generation might receive them. I enjoy those talks on the drive to and from school, and they have no idea how maniacally I talk to myself alone on the drive home. No matter the outcome of those discussions, my deepest hope is that they learn the value of pouring your heart into something, not because it promises a paycheck and a pension, but because it guarantees fulfillment. I think they'll see the value in this pursuit once I sell tens of copies of this book.

About the Author

Mark Brennan was born and raised in Cleveland, Ohio. He served five years in the Marine Corps and then attended the Virginia Commonwealth University, where he attained a Bachelor of Arts degree in English. Currently, he lives in North Carolina with his wife and two children. All things considered, he's a very, very cool guy. Everyone says so.

This is Mark's second publication, following the future-award-winning novel, The One and Only Fat Chance.